THE SECOND KEY

A

NOVEL

BY
CHERYL HOLDEFER

www.facebook.com/pages/Cheryl-Holdefer/132424563596673

Copyright ©2014 by Cheryl Holdefer
Cover design by Sarah Hansen
(http://www.okaycreations.com/)
Interior design and formatting by JT Formatting

ISBN-13: 978-0615975603

First Edition: March 2014
Library of Congress Cataloging-in-Publication Data

Holdefer, Cheryl
        The Second Key – 1st ed

To my children, Lauren and Ricky,
and to my husband, Dave.

Secrets

EVERYONE HAS THEIR secrets: the ones we are asked to guard for others, the ones we build on our own, and those we stumble upon unknowingly.

They may be the result of unbridled passion and fear of discovery, irrepressible greed or delicious deceit, or unrestrained lust for the control of person or circumstance. And yet, they may appear inadvertently out of nothingness, out of ignorance or misunderstanding, with not much consequence for anyone but our selves.

Nevertheless, we may happen upon one of these confidences quite by accident. Perhaps we have found a token, such as a key, that unlocks a truth. The contents become a concealed piece of our soul. They empower us with anonymity and influence on the one hand, and they burden us with an unwanted liability on the other.

It is when a secret has the potential to hurt others that we are faced with fundamental decisions revealing our true character: do we use the discovery for retribution or vindication? Do we pursue absolute truth and full disclosure to expose others' deficiencies in exchange for a few moments of personal satisfaction? To what cost?

Beware, for every secret has a hidden portal, and someone may find a second key...

Chapter 1

"*I AM SO done with dating*," Rachel exclaimed to her friend Darlene as they stood on the veranda overlooking the vineyards at Barrel Oak Winery.

It was an unseasonably warm Saturday afternoon in early December, and the winery was packed with people. Rachel liked this winery because they welcomed canine visitors, so she had brought her black Lab Oliver with her for the ride. Actually, Oliver had jumped onto the back seat of the car back home, and that was that. Coaxing him out with a dog treat didn't seem to work anymore.

"What do you mean you're *done with dating*? Come on, Rachel, you just *started* dating. And you've had like, what, four dates?"

"Three."

"*Three* dates in three years." Darlene chuckled and shook her head disapprovingly.

"I'm not looking for another husband, Darlene." She paused for a moment to take a sip of her wine. "You know Patrick was my soul mate, and I'm not going to find that again, so what's the point of searching?"

"The point is that life goes on, Rachel. Patrick is dead,

and you are not."

She felt bad the moment she had made the comment.

"Shit, I'm sorry. I didn't mean to be so blunt," Darlene said with a sigh. "But love *can* happen more than once, and it doesn't have to match what you had. It can be different. And it can be fulfilling. You just can't keep hiding from it, or it will never find you."

"I'm not hiding!"

"Yes you are. Patrick died three years ago and you haven't looked at another man since then. Not that I'm rushing you. But you are getting older," her friend said with an attempt to add humor to her previous remark.

"What?!"

"Rachel, all you do is work and clean house and take care of your sons and the dog. And that's all good stuff, but you barely go out anywhere with friends. I can't even get you to go to the movies with Anthony and me."

"I'm not going to get in the middle of that! You and Anthony are planning your wedding, and I'm not going to be a third wheel. And I *do* get out when I'm not so busy with the twins and work."

"Like what? Where have you gone this year that didn't involve your boys?"

"I go to plenty of places. I went to that winefest in October with Becky and Amber from work, remember? And I went to a couple of movies with Rhonda and Dorothy. Oh, and I went camping this past summer with my sister-in-law and her son and my boys in upstate New York, and we had a blast!"

"That's my point. You do mostly family things. And things with those friends of Patrick's from the military.

You need to distance yourself from that crowd, Rachel. Really. They just keep the whole Patrick thing alive; all those military wives like Dorothy and Rhonda and Jaclyn."

"It's kind of my support group, Darlene. Military wives stick together."

"But you aren't a military wife anymore, Rachel. Patrick is gone. The Air Force isn't a part of your life anymore."

Darlene wondered if she was being too rough on her friend. Things had to be said, though, and she wasn't going to hold back when she knew she was right.

Darlene was a gorgeous African-American woman in her late thirties who had been Rachel's friend for ten years. She had been there for her when Patrick died, and she would continue to be there for her friend until one of them fell off the ends of the earth. They both worked at the same high school in Hampton, Virginia, so they saw each other frequently. Darlene was the head of the counseling department, and Rachel was a Spanish teacher.

"Look, I don't pretend to comprehend what you have gone through," Darlene continued. "Your husband died in a tragic accident. You had a miscarriage right after that. You had to go through all that insurance crap resulting from Patrick's accident, and then you had to increase your hours from part-time to full-time at work while raising your twelve-year-old sons."

"Thirteen."

"What?"

"They're thirteen now."

"When did *that* happen?!"

They both laughed and it seemed to lighten the mood a

bit.

"You mentioned the baby," Rachel said pensively. "She wasn't meant to be, Darlene. I really do believe that. Just imagine if I had had to raise *three* children on my own. And a dog!"

Oliver looked up at her from the deck where they were standing and she petted him on the head to reassure him.

"And I *do* accept Patrick is gone and that it's about time I move on in the romance department. I'm working on it. It's just hard to not compare other men to him, you know? I don't deliberately try, anyway. Look, I had never met a man I couldn't live without until Patrick came along, and so far, I just haven't met another one like him."

"I know. Patrick was unique. Just keep trying to open up your heart to new experiences a little more each day; like the open heart on that necklace you've been wearing."

"It *is* open," Rachel responded defensively while unconsciously reaching for the dainty brass key she wore around her neck. She touched the open heart design at the bow of the key and then dropped it against her chest and exhaled.

"Okay," she said, extending her arms outward as if inviting someone in for an embrace, "look, I'm opening my heart. You see? No one out there wants me."

"I want you!" Darlene grabbed her friend and pulled her in for a big hug.

These courageous conversations were always difficult. Maybe it was time for another glass of wine. Or a bottle. A big one.

"I am trying, though, Darlene. I even joined that stupid online dating service last month so I could start looking for a date to take to that wedding of yours next summer," Rachel smiled and faked a big sigh for her friend's benefit. "You see what I do for you?"

"You are such a bull-shitter, girl! You didn't join that for me." Darlene nudged her friend. "You know you can come with that big old dog of yours as your date. We're not picky!"

They both laughed and looked down at Oliver as he lay there oblivious.

"Oliver may actually be a better date than some of those guys I've been chatting with online. I can't believe I let my sister-in-law convince me to sign up for this matchmaking thing last month. Actually, I'm betting it was really my brother Kevin who thought of it, but he sent Erin to persuade me to sign up. He's such a brat!"

"But he's a *good* brat!" her friend responded with a smile. "Now, give me the update. You told me last week you started chatting online with some guy who has five dogs, and then with some other guy that has a boat and wants to sail around the world. I hope you didn't agree to go out with that one, because you can't be sailing all over the world right now, mama."

"And five dogs would be a better choice?"

"Good point. So is there anyone else that looks like a prospect?"

"I don't know," she replied halfheartedly. "It *is* fun looking at all the profiles and pictures on the site, but once you start actually chatting with someone, they say they want to meet you in person."

"So?"

"It just feels like it goes so quick. One day you're saying hello, and the next day they say they want to meet you for coffee. Everybody is in such a hurry!"

"True. But you can't just chat on a computer forever, either."

"Because...?"

"Because that's not the real world, Rach. I mean, you hear those stories about people who carry on these long affairs online without meeting each other, and when they finally decide to meet, they find out the person they were chatting with wasn't really that person. So it's best to just meet the guy as soon as possible and see if he's who he says he is."

"What on earth are you talking about?"

"I read it in a magazine last month. There was a story about some pro-football player who met a girl on one of those matchmaking services, and they dated online for almost a year without ever meeting in person. Apparently they lived in different states. When he insisted on meeting her face-to-face to declare his love, he discovered his football buddies had created this fictitious girl and he had been the brunt of their jokes the whole year."

"Oh no!"

"Oh yes. She didn't exist. They had used photos of some cheerleader on another team, and the guys had been taking turns logging in as her and writing him love letters. It was so sad. It made national news, believe it or not, and all the night-time comedy shows on TV had a field day with it."

"Why didn't he insist on meeting her before that? I mean, a whole year, and they never wanted to meet each other?"

"He did want to meet her. In the magazine interview I read, he said he had tried to get together with her, but she had always had some excuse. Like one time she supposedly bought a plane ticket to go see him, but then she cancelled at the last minute saying her grandmother was ill or something. Apparently the excuses were all very credible, and the fact he was so busy playing in stadiums all over the place didn't help with scheduling a meet."

"Wow. Now you have my attention. That is scary." She paused for a few seconds as she thought about this new information.

"Okay, I wasn't going to tell you this," Rachel divulged as she shifted her stance nervously to face her friend, "but now I think I will. I went out on a date last night with one of the guys I've been chatting with for about two weeks."

"Are you kidding?! Girl, why weren't you going to tell me about it?"

"Because it didn't work out. I figured I'd just tell you when one of these dates turns into something worth talking about."

"There are others?"

"No, no, no! This was the first time I accepted to meet anyone."

"Well next time tell me. I need to know, 'cause I'm nosey like that. Here I am lecturing you about being a homebody, and you actually went out on a date. So why didn't it work out?"

"Okay, I'll tell you the story, but I'm going to need another glass of wine for this."

The sun was sliding behind a swelling cluster of clouds

and the wind was picking up its pace. It was time to go inside. Oliver was perfectly happy following them indoors and over to the counter where the proprietor kept a large plastic container of dog treats.

"Was it that bad?" Darlene asked while they waited for the pourer behind the counter to come their way.

"Well, a little freaky; kind of like your story about the football player."

"How so? Was he—"

"Oh, wait a sec," Rachel interrupted. "I see the Barrel Oak owners over there by the fireplace. I'll be right back. Don't order any wine yet. I want to see what Sharon and Brian recommend."

"You know them?"

"Kind of. Contrary to your belief that I never get out much, I do come here occasionally with Oliver and sit on the terrace with a glass of wine and a good book when the boys are off somewhere. I'm telling you, being out there in the fresh air surrounded by nature is the best medicine for the soul. Kind of makes me want to own my own winery someday; I'd just sit out on the deck and sip wine and read."

"Except you'd have to have big bucks to own a winery and you'd have to know a little about making wine. Just details, though. Don't let me interrupt your dream."

"Hey, maybe I'll hit the lottery someday!"

"Gotta actually play the lottery to win, Rach."

"Whatever!"

Rachel went over to the fireplace and spoke to the proprietors while her friend waited with the dog and secured a couple of stools at the bar. She returned a few minutes later with a dog biscuit in one hand and a bottle of wine in the other. Oliver stood quickly at the sight of his treat.

"A whole bottle?" Darlene asked. "What are you trying to do to me? Get me in trouble with Anthony?"

"Of course!" she responded with a sly smile. "Okay, so this is a barrel fermented chardonnay that won a silver medal in the San Francisco Chronicle International Wine Competition. It only sells by the bottle, though, not by the glass. We can cork it and take it home if we don't finish it."

"I'm not taking anything home. Pour that sucker!"

They both raised their glasses in a toast and drew a long sip while savoring the oaky vanilla of the medal-winning wine.

Rachel had taken a class on wine appreciation in the summer while the boys were away with their grandparents; not that she would ever have a chance to do anything with the knowledge she had acquired. Although maybe when the boys were older and went off to college, she could become a connoisseur and write articles for a magazine such as *The Wine Spectator* or *The Wine Enthusiast*. Or perhaps she could assist with pouring wines at a local winery.

"Yum," Rachel said licking her lips. "I wonder if they use American oak or French oak barrels for this. It must be French, because the finish isn't as spicy as with American oak fermentation."

"You are such a wine snob! Now get back to your story about the date you had last night," Darlene said leaning in for the scoop.

"Oh yeah. So his name was Kent. A nice name, right? But not such a nice guy."

"Keep going."

"Well, I had been talking to him online for almost two weeks, and then he said he wanted to meet me. I had decided in advance if I ever went out on one of these meet-and-greet things, I'd drive to the site myself and I'd go someplace where there would be plenty of people. It would be safe, you know?"

"Good. Safety is good."

"So I picked a restaurant not too far from work. In retrospect, I should have picked a café for a quick cup of coffee instead of a meal at a restaurant that could take forever to end. Anyway, he was supposed to meet me at the restaurant at about six o'clock. First of all, the drive there was the pits with the rush-hour traffic, so I was already annoyed at myself for having agreed to meet him at that time on a Friday. But I got there right on time. *He* didn't show up until 6:45! Can you believe that? On the first date?"

Rachel frowned as she recalled waiting at the table and trying not to appear embarrassed about being stood up.

"Girl, I would have left his sorry little self in a minute!"

"He finally arrived just as I was ready to leave. He had some half-baked story about work issues that detained him. I wasn't sure whether to believe him or not, but I decided to give him the benefit of the doubt, so I stayed."

"What did he look like? I mean, not that it would have made any difference if the guy was a jerk."

"He had described himself on his profile as tall, dark-haired, and good-looking. And he *was* good-looking, to his credit. But he was so freaking conceited about it. He talked all night about himself, which was a big turn-off right there. I don't think he even asked one question about me."

"What? The man should know the first date it is all about the woman! Didn't he ever read *Men Are From Mars and Women are From Venus?*"

"Okay, counselor, calm down. I'm sure it works both ways."

"No it doesn't."

"Anyway, he talked the whole time about his fancy car, his weight-training and work-outs, what he eats to stay in shape, the sports teams he loves, and how he has loads of money invested in some company whose name eludes me. He kind of lost me after talking about his work-outs."

"Is he rich, then?"

"Well, you'd think so by the way he was talking. Money doesn't matter to me, though."

Rachel had meant it. She had won a large suit against the trucking company in Bahrain whose truck driver had run through a red light and had ploughed into her husband's car killing him and another passenger in the car.

"But listen to this," Rachel continued. "He said he had just bought a house in Florida last month for his son who was moving down south to start a new job. I guess the son had graduated from college and had landed a job there. Anyway, Kent never flew to Florida to check out the house before purchasing it from the agent. I didn't say anything when he told me this, but who signs a contract to buy a house without ever seeing it?"

"Wow."

"Yeah, wow. Anyway, when the son moved into the house, he found all kinds of structural problems. Apparently the house had been built too close to some wetlands or something. He had bought the house for a real bargain thinking it was just a fixer-upper."

"Hmm. That doesn't say much about his common sense, does it?"

"No. But that wasn't what bothered me, Darlene."

"What do you mean?"

"Kent said he's looking for another house for his son to live in while he's sorting out the legal issues for the first house. He said he needs some immediate cash, like $10,000, for a down-payment on the second house. Then he said he's having difficulty getting his hands on that much cash with such short notice."

"I thought he had all kinds of investments."

"Right? But it was weird, because he said he needed to find a friend who would be willing to loan him the ten thousand right away until he could liquidate some of his assets. Then he looked at me. He asked if I was interested in an investment, Darlene."

"*Are you shitting me?!*"

"No, I'm not kidding! Isn't that *bizarre*? I thought it was pretty brash for the first date. I mean, we had been e-mailing each other for a couple of weeks, but that doesn't mean we were best friends who would ask each other for loans or anything. Not even *slightly* good friends!"

"Yeah, you need to just run away from that," her friend retorted.

"I did."

"What did you say to him to get away?"

"We had already finished dinner by that time, so I told him I was ready to leave and I'd pay for half of the check."

"Don't get me started on why you felt you needed to pay for half," she waved her hand in the air. "So did you just leave?"

"He couldn't believe I wanted to go. I told him I didn't think it was going to work out for us for another date, but he still wanted to go out again. He kept telling me the conversation about the loan had just been a joke and he really liked me. He apologized a hundred times. It wasn't a joke, though, Darlene."

"No, he wasn't right for you. He needs to learn some manners. I hope he doesn't take advantage of someone else who isn't as smart as you."

"Thanks; I hope he doesn't either. He was pretty persistent about going out again, though. And you know how I don't like hurting anyone's feelings. But I just couldn't trust the guy after that conversation."

"So how did you get rid of him?"

"I told him I didn't want to go out anymore because I'd realized I'm just not ready to date yet after my husband died." Rachel cringed as she said this. "It's kind of the truth. I guess it's okay to use that as an excuse, right? Am I being sacrilegious?"

"Look, you said whatever you needed to say to get away from that opportunist. Maybe Patrick was watching out for you from above, you know? Like maybe he knew this guy wasn't right for you."

"You think so?" She smiled at the thought of Patrick looking out for her from beyond.

They sat there in silence for a moment enjoying their wine as they watched a group of ladies decked out in shades of purple slowly approach the bar in their spiked heels with sprays of violets scattered throughout their hair. One in particular was wearing a faux diamond tiara and a sash pronouncing her as the *Bride-To-Be*.

"Let's change the topic," Rachel said as she turned her attention back to Darlene. "Let's talk about your wedding. How are the preliminary plans going?"

Darlene and Anthony had been living together for about two years, and they had recently decided it was time to make it official. Darlene told him she liked his last name, Patterson, so he had decided to give it to her as a Christmas gift. Once he had bought the ring, however, he had decided it would be too long to wait until December to propose. He didn't do too well with keeping surprises. So he proposed to Darlene on Thanksgiving Day by secretly placing the diamond ring in her *Mimosa*, and nearly choking his beloved when she chugged that last sip from the champagne flute. They were planning to get married in late August. By then maybe the weather would be a bit cooler, and she would have had the whole summer to concentrate on the plans and preparation for her big event.

"We want something for about a hundred people," Darlene responded.

"Any thoughts as to where?"

"Actually, yes, and that's one of the reasons I wanted you to meet me here today. We've been thinking about getting married at a winery. What do you think?"

"It sounds great! Were you thinking about this particular winery for the venue?"

"Yeah, but now that I'm here, it looks a little too small. We would need to have a place for a band to set up, and there would need to be a dancing area. We'd also need some big tables for the food. I guess we could ask if they set up tents for that kind of thing outside, right? After all, you seem to have connections with the owners, girlfriend."

"Sure, I'll ask them if you want. Hey, what about the winery just down the road from here? I think it's called The Lotus Winery. I haven't been there for a while, but I seem to recall it was pretty big."

"I thought about that one too, but I believe it's up for sale, so it may not be an option."

"For sale? I had no idea. What happened to the nice retired couple that bought it about ten years ago?"

"I think they retired again. I heard they have children and grandchildren in North Carolina, so I think they are moving down there to be with them."

"Do you have any other wineries in mind?"

"A few. Anthony and I got a book from the Tourism Office and took notes on some of the wineries around here. We're going to try looking around during the Christmas holidays when he can get a few days of leave from work. I'll have the two weeks off from school, so I'll start narrowing it down a bit."

"Sounds like a good plan."

"Hey, do you want to come and look at some of them with me? Free glass of wine! And my treat!"

Oliver lifted his head off the floor at the mention of a treat.

"A free glass of wine sounds wonderful! I'm in. Let me know when, though, because I'm taking the boys up to my parents' place in New York to go skiing for part of the holidays."

"Oh yeah, I forgot. When are you going again?"

"We're going to leave right after school gets out on Thursday afternoon before break. We'll drive to New York to spend the night at my brother and Erin's house, and then on Friday morning Erin and my nephew will continue the drive with us to the ski lodge for five days. My brother has to work, so he can't go with us, but he'll join us back at my parents' house in Syracuse for Christmas Eve."

"Sounds like fun! You couldn't catch me dead on skis, though. Skis and I don't get along. I think if God had intended for me to strap a set of two-by-fours on my feet and hurl myself down a mountain, He would have given me a nice set of wings as well!"

Rachel shook her head and laughed.

"It'll be nice to have all three of the cousins together, though. My brother's son Brad is only a year older than my boys, and they're really close. Especially after Patrick died; my boys love spending time with family."

"So when will you get back?"

"We'll spend Friday through Wednesday morning at the lodge, and then Wednesday through Saturday morning at mom's house. On Saturday we'll head back home. I guess that only leaves Sunday and Monday for me to get together with you if you wanted to visit some wineries. We do have that Monday off, don't we?"

"Yes, but don't even worry about trying to get together. You'll probably need a rest after the trip. You'll *definitely* need time to unpack and do laundry. I'll go ahead and get a head start with Anthony on the locations, and I'll fill you in when you get back."

Darlene raised her glass for a toast. "Only three more weeks 'til winter break!"

"Three more weeks!" Rachel repeated.

Chapter 2

BACK HOME AFTER listening to Darlene talk about her wedding plans, Rachel thought about her own wedding and her nine years of marriage to Patrick before he was unexpectedly taken away from her.

Rachel had grown up in northern New York with her mom and dad in a modest home with quite the normal family. She had one older brother, Kevin, and two cats. When it was time for college, she had applied to and been accepted at the University of Virginia. She had wanted to go south for college, somewhere a little warmer, and her grandfather had encouraged her to apply to UVA since it was his *alma mater*. He had been excited at the prospect of having his granddaughter attend his old school because it would give him an excuse to go to the Cavaliers' football games while visiting her.

This was where Rachel Hayes had met Patrick Matthews. They had started dating during her sophomore year, even though he had been two years older than her and was in his last year of college.

Patrick had grown up in nearby Charlottesville. He had applied to the University of Virginia in order to join their

Air Force ROTC program after being a cadet at his local high school. He had wanted to be a pilot ever since he was four years old, his adoptive parents had said, so he had planned his future well and had stayed on course. That was who he was.

When they started dating, it had seemed an unlikely situation. Patrick would be graduating within the year and would be off to boot camp, and then he'd have to go to Corpus Christie in Texas for his training to be a pilot. Who knew where he would end up after that?

Rachel had wanted to be a Spanish teacher, and maybe move back to New York City to teach underprivileged children. However, she had fallen deeply in love with Patrick and knew without a doubt this was the person with whom she wanted to spend the rest of her life. She was willing to make the sacrifices, whatever they would be, so she could be with him forever. She had never suspected forever would translate into nine short years.

After Patrick's graduation from UVA, he went to the Camp Lejeune military training facility in Jacksonville, North Carolina, and then on to Texas as expected. Rachel had stayed back at the university finishing up her degree in education.

The couple saw each other intermittently for those two years and at one point Rachel had asked herself if Patrick was truly the person she should marry. She hadn't doubted her love, but she had wondered if he would still be the same person two years after having had a totally different life experience in the military.

She had also had to consider he would be traveling quite a bit as a helicopter pilot, probably to war zones whose names she couldn't even pronounce, and she would likely become a solitary military wife in one of those unknown countries with no hope of ever seeing a McDonald's or ever watching a television program in English. Was she cut out for that? Or was she just being an ignorant American?

Rachel debated having to give up her dream to become a teacher. The last two years of her degree in Education had inspired her, and she had eagerly yearned to become a teacher with her own classroom and her own kids.

After much thought, however, she determined Patrick was her future, and she would do whatever it took to be with him. Not many people could claim finding the love of their life, and she was not about to give up hers.

When she graduated from UVA, Rachel had assumed they would get married right away; at least that is what Patrick had been saying in his letters. But Patrick's career goals had changed, or had been changed for him, and he had needed more training for a new direction involving intelligence surveillance. He had explained to her it would be best to delay the wedding another two years until he could complete the training program that would take him to remote places for long periods of time.

During the years following her graduation, Rachel began substituting in local high schools in Charlottesville while living with Patrick's parents and attending graduate school in the evenings. She had decided she might as well go for her Master's Degree since she would have a couple of years of waiting before becoming Mrs. Matthews. It was better to get the degree at that point rather than try to piece it together while travelling from military base to military base later on.

Patrick finally came home two years later and broke the news to Rachel and his parents that he would be permanently stationed at Langley Air Force Base in Hampton, just a little over two hours southeast from where his parents lived in Charlottesville.

Patrick received his commission as an Air Force Pilot and started working at the Intelligence Surveillance and Reconnaissance Wing at Langley AFB. It was one of the oldest facilities of the Air Force established by Pierpont Langley in 1916 prior to America's entry into World War I. Patrick had been torn about not being a Black Hawk, as he had originally wanted, but Rachel was relieved he would be stationed at the base behind a solid wooden desk rather than out in the perilous skies. He would still need to travel at times, he had explained, but he would be based in Hampton where they could get married, settle down, and buy a house. Rachel would be able to start applying to schools for a teaching position, and they could even think about having children one day. It was perfect.

Patrick officially proposed to Rachel when he returned to Charlottesville that year, and they got married shortly thereafter in a small military ceremony on the base with their families present. Rachel found a job as a Spanish teacher at a local high school in Hampton, and they purchased a comfortable three-bedroom home nearby. It had a spacious back yard for a dog they would surely adopt someday to keep the Matthews children company. Rachel had wanted plenty of those. Children, not dogs.

Two years into their marriage, Rachel and Patrick had become proud parents of twin boys: Brandon and Andrew.

They had named one after her father, Brandon, and the other after his father, Andrew. Rachel had been able to reduce her hours to half-time at the high school so she could be home as much as possible with the boys. They had also adopted Oliver that year, and the children grew up chasing him around the yard, yanking on his tail, trying to eat his dog food, and laying on the floor with him as they watched their cartoons on television.

Rachel reminisced about the days she and Patrick had strolled through the park with the two baby carriages, progressing to bike riding, camping out, and trips to the beach once the twins were old enough to enjoy them. There were sand dollars and conch shells on every shelf in the house to remind them of their wonderful adventures. They had even gone to Disney World for the boys' seventh birthday and had made friends with all the animated characters they had met in the park.

Patrick's job had required him to travel to undisclosed locations every now and then, and Rachel had learned not to ask too many questions regarding those assignments. She had always packed for him and had made sure the family got together for quality time the night before his trips abroad. Their favorite thing to do the evening before a trip had been to order pizza and watch home movies. Those evenings had always been full of laughter, wrestling on the floor with the boys and Oliver, and chocolate sprinkles everywhere. Sprinkles from the ice-cream sundaes, that is.

Rachel's mood changed as she thought about the last weeks of her idyllic life and marriage to her husband. She recollected how Patrick's last tour of duty had come up so unexpectedly; the one that had ended all those good times they had had as a family of four. Patrick had come home on a Thursday evening asking for his passport and reporting he would be leaving on Saturday morning. He would be gone for a week. Rachel had been upset because the boys had asked their dad to come to their first Little League baseball game that Saturday, and he had promised he would schedule his work around the game and would be there to watch them. They had also planned to take a few days off the following week during spring break to go on a road trip to Washington DC to visit the monuments and museums along the mall near the capitol building. Rachel remembered arguing with Patrick about the sudden assignment because it had seemed like he had been traveling more than usual. He had returned from a trip only one month prior to that one, after which he had reassured her he would spend more time at home.

She had known her husband's job demands would be unpredictable. He had warned her, and she had been on board with it; at least superficially. It was the military, after all. How could she argue against protecting the country? So when he told her about the pending obligation, she had reluctantly accepted it and had considered taking the boys to Washington on her own. But Patrick had promised to make it up to her and the twins when he returned from Bahrain, and had convinced her to postpone the trip to the capitol for another time.

On the Friday evening prior to the trip, Patrick's friend Eric, an Air Force colleague from Langley, had invited the two of them over to dinner at his house. Eric had also been assigned to the special operation in Bahrain, and his wife Dorothy had wanted to put together an impromptu dinner party for the two couples and some of their friends from their unit. Rachel had objected because she had wanted Patrick to spend the evening with the boys at home as was their tradition; he'd have plenty of time to be with his coworkers overseas. Nonetheless, she had conceded and had gone to the dinner event at Eric's house.

The party had created friction between Rachel and her husband and it had raised questions in her mind about their marriage; questions that still lingered. They would surface every now and then when she'd quietly review the pages of her last days and moments with Patrick. She would always try to turn that particular page quickly, however, not wanting to remember much about it.

Patrick had practically begged her to go to the dinner at Eric's, but she had never understood why it had been so important to have her there, since he had practically ignored her the entire evening. He had spent hours surrounded by his buddies drinking heavily, smoking cigars, and laughing at whatever outrageous quips all the women in the room had been barred from hearing. Rachel had not been happy about it at all. And yet, after his death, she had felt pangs of guilt and wondered how she could have ever wanted to deprive him of those last moments of pleasure on this earth with his friends.

Rachel recollected how the guests sitting at the dinner table that evening had been totally enthralled by Patrick's hypnotic tales of his exploits. So much so, she had felt as if she had been an interloper lured in by the adventures of a stranger. She remembered looking around the table and watching the guests riveted to Patrick's expressive face as he shared the detailed sketches of his trips to the Middle

East. There had been enthusiastic approval and admiration. It occurred to her she hadn't heard half of the anecdotes he had been telling that evening, and she had wondered why. It wasn't as if he had been sharing covert information in his stories, so why hadn't he ever shared them with her? She would have venerated him as much as his contemporaries seated at the table. Had she not been receptive enough when he came home from his excursions, enough for him to tell her a few tales at their own dinner table?

In her darkest moments after his death, Rachel wondered if she had been too busy with the details of her own life and hadn't been accessible enough to the needs of her husband. Maybe that was why she hadn't heard about his ventures. Maybe he had been trying to capture her attention, but she had been too selfishly absorbed in her own minutiae. It could have been her fault, not his, for growing apart.

Had we been growing apart?

Rachel had predicted the evening at Eric's house would not end well, but she had kept quiet until they returned home, so as not to embarrass him or lead his friends to believe there could be difficulties in the marriage.

She remembered coming home afterwards and arguing well into the night about the sacrifices she had made, about his broken promises, and about him choosing to go to the party instead of staying at home with the boys his last evening before the trip. She told him she had known fully what she had signed up for when she had agreed to marry a military man; she just hadn't realized her husband's pledge to the Air Force would have been so significantly stronger than to his commitment to his family.

Was I wrong to question his loyalty?

There had been a time when his world had revolved around her, and she had told him during the argument that she longed for that time again. He had written her hundreds of letters when he had been on his earlier missions, had surprised her with flowers every now and then, and had purchased beautiful little trinkets for her from the places he had visited on his tours. He had left her Post-It notes with smiley faces stuck to the mirror in the bathroom so when she woke up and brushed her teeth, she'd see he had thought about her. He'd have made the coffee and had her cup ready to go on the counter when she came downstairs in the mornings each day. And most significantly, their lovemaking had been passionate and enduring and full of promise when he had returned from his trips, as if he couldn't get enough of her smell and her taste.

But somewhere along the line, Patrick had seemingly changed. Or had it been her? Had she become a mundane wife who complained too much about her husband's long hours at work, his inattentiveness, and his fragmented promises? Had she been wrong to expect him to take out the trash, to replace the light bulb in the laundry room, or to remember to take the dog to the groomer for a bath? Had she let herself go and become an unappealing nag who had worn sweat pants one time too many?

Oh, God, did I become too comfortable in my role as a wife and forget I was a woman and he was a man?

She wasn't naïve enough to believe amorous eroticism, the type of desire reserved for honeymooners, could endure an entire marriage. But certainly there should be thoughtfulness and compassion, time together holding hands, kissing to say good morning and hugging to say good-night. And *some* kind of sex. It may not have been as ardent as before, but she had certainly felt passion for him.

Did he feel the same?

Rachel recalled sensing Patrick had seemed preoccupied several weeks before his last trip. She would catch him at home gazing off into space while watching TV, or distracted while listening to the boys at the dinner table; not recollecting a word they had said. She had questioned him, but it had been difficult to get him to talk about his thoughts. She had assumed most military men were like that before any significant commission. Talking about feelings may have translated into vulnerability at a time when he had needed to be focused and strong for the impending tour of duty. Her husband certainly couldn't afford to be emotionally exposed in his line of work.

Rachel thought again about the night they had quarreled following the dinner party, and the point at which they had finally unloaded all that had been pent up in their hearts. She remembered feeling exhausted and empty of words. But it had been cathartic; healthy for them both. They had begun the evening speaking in loud accusatory voices with her crying desolately, but they had eventually ended the argument with renewed hope in their love and commitment to regenerate their relationship.

In retrospect, the anger that evening could have been a result of her frustration just as much as it had been of confusion, Rachel had decided. She had been frustrated at the thought of having to be alone again for an undisclosed time; to have to take care of the leak behind the toilet and the broken handrail on the stairway; to mulch the spring garden by herself; to try to do something fun with the kids over their spring break; to make excuses to the family and friends for cancelled events; and to have to watch old movies by herself at night on the couch with the dog and a bag of pistachios for comfort.

Nevertheless, their dispute had come to an impasse. Neither had been right, and neither had been wrong. Feelings had been acknowledged and apologies made. They had prepared for bed after repeated assurances to spend more time together. They had vowed to go on a vacation when Patrick returned, just the two of them, to some exotic island in the Caribbean. While he was gone, Rachel would dedicate time to looking online for different vacation packages and would let him know what she had found when he returned. He had told her to buy some pretty sundresses for their romantic escape, and he'd promised her he would put in for leave from work as soon as he had returned from the trip to Bahrain. They had agreed to postpone the spring trip to Washington DC until the summer so they could all go as a family. He would make a list of the places to visit, such as the Space Museum and the Spy Museum, the White House, and the Smithsonian Museum of Natural History.

They had rekindled their spirits while making plans for the future and all had seemed well in the world once again. Every piece fit perfectly into the puzzle as she had envisioned it when she had married her husband on that beautiful spring day nine years prior to that evening. So much so, that Patrick had asked Rachel if she had still wanted to try to have a baby girl.

Rachel had been ecstatic by the offer to add to their family. Patrick had not wanted to have any more children, but Rachel had always wanted to try once more for a little girl to add to their brood. They had decided that evening there would be no reason to wait until his return from Bahrain. What the heck; it could happen that night. The thought of adding another child to the family had made their love-making more vibrant and intense than it had been for a very long time. It had been with this revived love they had been able to say good-bye once more before the last trip Patrick would ever make.

Chapter 3

"ANDREW! BRANDON! DO you have your suitcases ready? We have to hit the road in fifteen minutes if we're going to make it to New York in time for dinner at your Aunt Erin's house!"

It was Thursday afternoon, an early release day from school, and the beginning of winter break for all three of them. They were headed to Rachel's brother's house in New York for the night, and then on to their much awaited ski trip to Lake Placid. They had stayed up late the previous night packing suitcases, taking the dog to the kennel, leaving instructions for the neighbor to get the mail and newspapers, and packing snacks for their five-hour road trip.

"Mom," Andrew yelled down the stairs, "do you know where my ski gloves are? I can't find them."

"I already packed them, buddy. Don't worry; I've got everything on the list. And if we forget something, we'll buy it!"

"You always say that, mom," Brandon replied coming into the foyer from the garage. "So what if I forget my *head,* huh?" They both laughed as Rachel ruffled her son's longish brown hair.

Brandon was about three minutes older than Andrew. They were fraternal twins, thank God, so it was easy to tell them apart. Although they looked nothing like each other (Brandon was a bit taller with brownish hair and green eyes, and Andrew had dark blonde hair and brown eyes), they had similar character traits and interests. Both were kind and respectful, and they were mature for their thirteen years. Rachel didn't know if that early maturity came from the gene pool or from them stepping up to fill their dad's shoes after he had died. They were both not only smart, they had good common sense. In school, Brandon excelled in math and Andrew was drawn to the sciences. Neither liked Spanish, which was what Rachel taught in high school. Oh well, she didn't like science or math either. They both ate just about anything, making it easy for her to cook meals. They also enjoyed the same activities and sports. The boys played soccer in the fall, skied in the winter, and participated in baseball in the spring. They even played the same position in baseball: third base. So what does one do if one has sons who play the same position? Don't enroll them on the same team. That's how life gets complicated. Rachel would go to two games, three times per week, at different times and different fields. When the boys played on the same day at the same time, she would have to drive to one field for half of one game, and rush to the other field for the second half of the other game. It was great when their teams occasionally played against each other on the same field. Or was it? Choosing which side to sit on at the game was an issue, and selecting what team colors to wear made it impossible to dress appropriately when wearing orange and blue for Andrew's team, and green and yellow for Brandon's team on the same day. Might as well plug her in and call her a Christmas tree.

"Okay, are we ready now?" she asked one more time as she ushered them out the front door and over to the car with their suitcases and backpacks.

"You guys have your IPods? How about the laptop to watch movies on the way up? And snack bags? Oh, what about your toothbrushes?" she asked while turning to go back into the house.

"Mom, we're all set! And if we forgot something, we can buy it!" They all laughed.

HALF AN HOUR later Rachel settled into the drive and stopped obsessing over the list of things she had wanted to pack for the trip. The boys were right; if they didn't have it, they would do without, or they would borrow whatever it was from their cousin. Or buy it.

Andrew had fallen asleep in the back seat. He had complained about not feeling well, so she made a mental note to have him see a doctor when they got back from the trip. He had been feeling tired a lot lately. Maybe she was running the boys ragged with all the sports activities and now this trip. She hoped he was not getting the flu and would be okay for the trip. Being out in the cold all day on a ski slope was probably not the best thing if he was coming down with a virus. She'd have to keep an eye on him.

Stop worrying, she told herself.

Brandon was watching a DVD on his laptop in the front seat, and Rachel glanced over every now and then at the screen when she heard him chuckle at the funny parts of the movie. He looked so much like his father. He even had his same way of snickering when something was funny.

Patrick. She thought back to when he had said good-bye to her at the airport and had chatted about plans for the Caribbean vacation they would take when he returned from Bahrain. He had told her at the airport to wear the gift he had given her the year before at Christmas, the small brass key with the open heart on it. He told her not to take it off until he returned, and that when he did, he would fill the heart with all of his love; love she alone would have for the rest of their lives. It had been one of the last gifts she had received from him.

Saying good-bye to Patrick had been tough that day. It had always been sad when she had taken him to the airport. But this time had been different. This time she had felt as if they had renewed their vows and had taken the first steps on a path towards a magnificent journey. She had been anxious to begin spending more time with him doing the things they had talked about the previous evening. She'd make more exciting meals. She'd nag him less. She would be sure to wear make-up and nicer clothes when he was home. The grey sweatpants would go in the trash. Well, maybe she'd save them for working out in the gym. She would make sure to set aside every Friday night for a date night, whether that meant going out to dinner or a movie, or staying at home with him snuggled on the couch with popcorn and a glass of wine.

When she had returned home after taking Patrick to the airport for his trip, she had rushed straight up the stairs to her bedroom to look in her jewelry chest for the blue velvet box where she had kept her tiny brass key on a golden chain. Patrick had anticipated she would, and he had left a small handwritten note tucked into the top of the box that morning. She had slowly opened the box to take out the treasure and then she read his note:

Thank you for always bringing me back and reminding me how much you mean to me. I love you with all my heart and I hope you will forgive me and let me back into yours.
Love,
Patrick

Rachel remembered holding the delicate box in both hands for a long moment, and then kissing the note Patrick had penned a few short hours before leaving. She had felt his love; she had imagined his smile as she had thought about him hiding the note. As the tears fell from her eyes that day, she had silently thanked God for helping them reconcile the previous night. She had asked that Patrick be delivered home safely from Bahrain the following week.

Rachel remembered fastening the clasp of the chain around her neck and thinking she would keep it there until Patrick came home, just as she had promised him.

But Patrick never came home. He would never see her open heart waiting for his love.

Chapter 4

THE DRIVE TO Kevin and Erin's house on Thursday evening was fairly smooth with not too much traffic in spite of the beginning of rush hour. Both boys were asleep in the car, so Rachel turned off the radio and decided to take advantage of the quiet time to sort through her thoughts about the whole dating issue she and Darlene had been talking about at the winery.

She wondered if anyone could ever replace Patrick. Darlene seemed to think so. But it was scary, because Patrick had been the only person Rachel had ever slept with, the only person she had fallen in love with, and the only person who had truly understood her.

It had been a long time since she had been in the dating arena, and the few dates she did have had turned out to be a bust. It was discouraging. The latest guy had been so self-absorbed and just plain weird. *Ten thousand dollars?* Really? The other two dates she had been on hadn't fared any better. One had been a blind date a friend had set her up with, and he had been nice enough, but had been too old. Sixteen years apart was too much. What should the age range be? Five years? Ten? Another guy she had met at the

Teacher's Convention in October had been a little too morose for her, but it had taken her three dates to realize it; three dates too many. There would have to be rules about that: know the guy in one date. Either you like him, or you don't. He had been a cynic and had spun every subject they had debated through a web of despair and gloom. He had miserably criticized the government, health care, welfare, the teacher's union, administrators, and even the institution of marriage. Everything was everyone else's fault. People were too this or too that. Rachel certainly hadn't wanted the burden of figuring out what it would take to brighten his life. Nope, not her job. Bye-bye morose man.

Eons ago, she had dated a few nice guys in high school, but she had not taken those relationships seriously because she had been focused on going to college and hadn't wanted to be tied down when she had left. She wondered what had happened to those guys. Had they gotten married too? She couldn't even remember their names now.

How does someone even *meet* men to date? Rachel wasn't the type to hang out in bars. There weren't any unmarried male teachers in her building at work who interested her. There was one single father on Brandon's baseball team, but he didn't really seem interested in her. He was probably already taken. Or maybe he was gay. Rachel had a close gay friend who she spent time with every now and then, but he didn't have any single friends interested in women. So where should she go? Someone had recommended bookstores, but who had time to go sit in a *Barnes and Noble* pretending to read some Albert Camus classic while the boys were at home clamoring for dinner? Heck, there wasn't even any time in her crazy schedule to go on dates, so what was the point of worrying about it?

Maybe when the boys go off to college...

Rachel recalled having felt so empty after losing Patrick. She didn't think she could go through another loss if she were to fall in love again someday and then be rejected. And yet, rejection was one thing, and losing a spouse to death was totally different. It tore at every part of the soul, slashing at the heart until the unbearable pain left only numbness. She had been told there was recovery after losing a spouse. One could still find purpose, whether it be raising the children left behind, volunteering at a hospital or a school, or working with a humanitarian or political organization. She knew she had survived because of her children. She was happy she had both of her boys, and they were both healthy. She didn't think she could endure losing one of *them*.

But Darlene was right when she had said it was time to live in the present and to move forward, for the sake of her children if not for herself. *Make time in your schedule,* she had said. *It might be healthy for the boys to see their mother excited about something or someone.* Not that she sulked around the house or anything; but her happiness always stemmed from what the boys were doing. They were in the eighth grade now, and they'd be leaving for college in about four years. Surely they would want to see her happy before they were gone. They certainly wouldn't want the liability of having to stick around to make her happy, right? Hadn't she just said that about the pessimistic guy she had met in October at the convention? Not wanting to be responsible for making him happy? Well, it worked for children and their parents too.

She hoped the boys would approve of her dating someone. *Should she ask them if it is okay?* Wait a minute; she's the parent. She wouldn't ask. But she'd be discreet and make sure she knew the guy well before bringing him home. She'd have the FBI run a background check on him. Rachel smiled at the thought, and yet, she knew she would have to be certain any new contender would be someone her boys could tolerate, and maybe even like. They didn't have to love him or call him dad, but they'd have to approve of him for their mom. They'd have to trust him to take care of her and make her happy; that she knew.

Okay, she concluded. She'd start dating. She felt slightly invigorated thinking about the possibility of allowing herself to date again, but also somewhat fearful of the unknown. More like terrified, actually. So what if this Kent guy was just a wrong match? There are plenty of others. But would the good ones be attracted to her? She wasn't ugly by any stretch of the imagination, at least that's what Darlene had told her. And she felt like she was smart enough to discuss a broad spectrum of topics from politics to sports to health care and the stock market. What else did guys talk about? She was athletic enough; she skied down the Black Diamond slopes with her sons in the winter, and she consistently ran five miles several times each week. So was she marketable enough?

Darlene had told her about a year after Patrick's death that people who wallowed in their adversities would never attract any friends, or dates, for that matter, because it made them unappealing. She had told her to shape up her attitude and slap on some make-up. That Darlene; she could really tell it like it is. Rachel knew her attitude towards life had changed over the past two years. It had taken some time, but she had landed in a comfortable place. Even though she had felt extreme pain and loss, she had never felt sorry for herself and had never worn her loss like a medal. She knew someone's death or illness was not meant to be a medal for the one left behind; there was no need to stagger, make excuses, or place blame for life's misfortunes. She could either pick up the pieces and make her way, or stumble through a hapless life; it was up to her. So she had gathered the pieces, glued them together, and life became good again. Not perfect, but good.

Perfect is overrated. Perfect means done; finished. And then what is there?

THE BOYS WOKE up briefly and Rachel decided to pull into a rest stop so they could stretch their legs and use the bathrooms. She needed some coffee, too.

They got back on the road and the twins quickly resumed their naps. She remembered how as a kid she used to fall asleep on road trips as well; the motion of the car just did that to her.

As a truck passed her on the turnpike, about an hour from her brother's house, Rachel's thoughts wandered once more to Patrick. She recalled the day she received the news her husband had been involved in the accident. She knew it was counterproductive to review that day in her mind, especially since she had wanted to begin a new chapter in her life, but she figured she'd open that mental file one more time before filing it in the rear of the cabinet to make room for a new one up front. The old file would be named *Yes-*

terday. She would name the new file *Today*. *Today* would be the beginning of her next life; a life full of hope. She'd open her heart, just as Darlene had told her to do. *If you open up your heart,* she had said, *love will come when you least expect it; you won't have to search for it.* She was hoping her friend was right on this. She'd buy her a pizza if she was. Not the thin kind; the gooey thick cheesy kind. Rachel smiled and felt the pangs of hunger begin.

Dinner in one more hour, she thought.

It had been a sunny spring day, Rachel reminisced, when she had received the news about Patrick's death. It was a Thursday, and Patrick had been scheduled to return from Bahrain the following day. She had planned a lovely Easter weekend that would start with dinner at their favorite restaurant on Friday, the boys' baseball games on Saturday morning, dyeing the eggs for Easter in the afternoon, and then going to a movie they had all wanted to see for weeks. After the boys would have gone to sleep, she would have spent time with Patrick preparing the Easter baskets for them. At ten years old, they had probably been a little old for Easter baskets, but it had been a tradition she had still cherished. She loved decorating for all the holidays, and she loved giving her boys little presents and surprises. Easter had always been one of her favorite holidays, and she had enjoyed cooking a big honey ham and all the fixings for the dinner with the family. She had invited Patrick's parents over for the Easter dinner on Sunday. She and Patrick had had this tradition of getting up early on Easter morning and eating a cinnamon roll for breakfast while putting out the Easter baskets and hiding a few of the eggs in the living room. There would always be one egg for each boy with money in it, and those eggs would be the hardest ones to find. Patrick had enjoyed hiding them. When his job was done, he'd make some *Mimosas* and they'd spend a little time together out on the deck before the boys woke up.

I miss those times so much, she reflected.

On that particular Thursday, Rachel had been working in the front yard planting some flowers so the garden would look nice when Patrick was to return home from his trip. The boys had been over at a friend's house enjoying one of their last days off from school before their spring break was over. Rachel recollected having looked up momentarily from her gardening and having seen a black military car turn the bend and drive into their cul-de-sac. Her instincts had told her the car would stop in front of her house. *No,* she had thought to herself, *they were not there for her. They couldn't be there for her. Patrick was coming home the next day, and everything would be okay.* She remembered returning to her gardening, refusing to pay any attention to the intruders.

Nonetheless, the car had stopped in front of her house. Rachel recalled having lifted her head just enough from the flower bed to catch the car door opening. Then the polished black shoes had stepped out onto the sidewalk. She could still see them headed in her direction. They had approached in slow motion. *No,* she had thought, *this was a mistake! Patrick had a safe job and he was coming home.*

She remembered she had run into the house and had quickly slammed the door to shut out the sight of the black sedan. She could still hear the sound of their heavy boots advancing on the wooden porch, and then the ominous sound of the doorbell. She had not wanted to answer it, and she had waited quietly leaning against the wall by the side of the door in hopes the officers would go away. *They had no business being there,* she had thought. She had wished Patrick were home to handle whatever news the people were delivering. *He had always been the level-headed one in the family. He would have known what to do.* But the men in their razor-pleated slacks and starched white shirts had waited on the porch.

She couldn't remember opening the door. It hadn't been her turning the knob; *or had it?* Rachel recalled feeling as if her spirit had scampered away behind the door as her body had dutifully stayed to listen to the news delivered by the two officers. Their voices had been garbled. She hadn't been able to understand exactly what they had been saying; something about Patrick being pronounced dead on arrival at a hospital after a collision the previous evening in a small town in Bahrain. Rachel's soul had continued observing the scene from behind the door as the lifeless body nearby had stood frozen in the doorway not knowing what to do next. *She had to protect the body.* She remembered rushing from behind the door and yelling at the officers to get off her porch. She had called them liars and had spit at their feet, and she had tried to hit the dreadful monster who had been doing all the talking. *How dare they come to her house at Easter, this holy time, with such blasphemy?*

He's coming home tomorrow, she had cried to them. *You'll have to talk to him tomorrow!*

The officers had stood there calmly trying to get her to go inside the house. One had taken Rachel by the arm and had led her into the living room. It was there Rachel had felt her body merge with her mind and she had understood what the officers had been telling her. The first officer had grabbed her just in time as she had fainted and nearly hit the floor.

THE MEMORIAL HAD been held two weeks later. Patrick had wanted to be cremated, so there had been no rush in making the preparations for a quick viewing and funeral. The family had had some time to let things sink in, as much as they could, and then arrange for the church service and ceremony. There had been so much to organize, and Rachel had been overwhelmed. Arlington National Cemetery, where he would be inurned, had needed time to arrange for the ceremony as well. The cemetery typically had twenty five funerals every day, they had explained, and scheduling Patrick's interment would take a little time.

Rachel had been glad Patrick's parents lived nearby and had stepped in to help as much as they could even while grieving the loss of their only son. They had adopted Patrick when he was a baby, and he had been their son to the end; no one else's. Patrick had investigated and found his biological family when he was in college, but he had contacted them only to get his medical records; nothing more. He had needed the background information for the Air Force's health evaluation and security check. He had agreed to meet his biological mom to get her records, and it had been a short visit. He had learned his mom and dad had never married, and his mom had given him up for adoption because she had not had the means to care for him. His biological grandfather had been the one to mail him his father's records, as his father had died of a drug overdose shortly after Patrick was born.

When the body came back from Bahrain on the military aircraft, Rachel had not gone to the airport to retrieve it. She had not been able to muster the courage to receive her husband's remains. Patrick's parents had understood, and they had gone to meet the aircraft without her. They had known how much she had loved him.

Rachel had never figured her husband would die this way, so young, with the perfect family, the promising career, and Easter dinner waiting for him. She remembered focusing on details, such as who was going to decorate the Easter eggs with her, and how Patrick would know she was keeping her promise to wear his necklace every day. Her details led to larger questions such as who would be attending the eighth grade graduation for the boys. What about high school graduation? And college? She knew now those questions had been irrelevant and superficial, but they had been important details she had focused on when she hadn't been able to accept the greater picture of a future without him. She had had to focus on details. Laundry. Easter. Getting the boys ready for school the next week. Watering the lawn and her garden so the flowers would bloom.

The immediate family had arranged for a small church service in Patrick's honor at the Unitarian Church nearby prior to the interment the following day. Hundreds of well-wishers had shown up at the church to offer their condolences, prayers and support; so many more than she had expected. She had seen friends from her workplace, Langley Air Force Base, college, the neighborhood, and she had met family members she hadn't even known existed. They had all been very sympathetic. Rachel remembered she had hugged so many people that she had felt weak and almost unable to stand. But she had gotten through the first hurdle at the church by hanging close to her parents and depending on Patrick's parents to stick with the boys. After the church service, the family had gone home to eat all the wonderful food the neighbors and friends had dropped off earlier. Rachel remembered she hadn't been able to eat a thing. All she had wanted to do was throw up. Or go to her room to lay in bed until the night came, and then the morning, and then the night again.

Patrick's family had taken care of most of the details of the funeral for the following day. Rachel and the twins, and Patrick's parents and her own, had been driven to Arlington National Cemetery in a long black limousine. It had been a long drive from their home, but it had been her husband's wish to be inurned in the Columbarium at Arlington, so no one had complained about the distance. The cemetery had been the resting place for military casualties since 1864, and Rachel had been told that Patrick had earned the honor of resting there for eternity.

When they had arrived at the cemetery, a military chaplain had been there to greet them. The family had carried the urn with them containing the cremated remains. Rachel remembered thinking it was quite heavy. She had felt as if all her life's dreams had been added to its burden.

Rachel's memory of the military ritual had become a bit blurred over the years. She recalled having been given a mild sedative to calm her nerves after Patrick's death, so she had probably been in a medically-induced haze for some of the ceremony at Arlington. There were parts she could still remember vividly, however, such as the firing party and the bugler who had played Taps. Her clearest memory was of her sons towards the end of the ceremony. Brandon had walked up to the urn and had put both his little hands on it. He had laid his head on his hands, and had whispered *Good-bye, Daddy, I love you.* Andrew had run up to him and had hugged him from behind. Neither boy had cried at that moment, but she could remember seeing their lips and chins quiver. They had been real little men, the way their father would have wanted. She remembered Andrew walking Brandon back to his spot beside their mom.

When the chaplain had concluded the service and had backed away, the rifle volley had been initiated. *Bang! Bang! Bang!* The boys had continued standing there holding hands as the shots had fired loudly into the sky. Rachel remembered seeing their little bodies shake with each shot. Then there had been silence. A moment later the bugler had played *Taps* to signal the beginning of Patrick's last long sleep, as they had called it, and then the bugler had saluted them. At that point Rachel had fallen into her chair with her head in her hands and had cried uncontrollably. The boys had hovered over her back hugging her and sobbing with her.

Four soldiers had stepped over to the flag that had been donated by the Veteran's Administration, and they had begun folding it into an impressive tight and smooth triangle by the time Rachel had uncovered her face from her hands. Rachel remembered the sound of the flag being folded and creased by the white gloved hands as she had looked on from her chair. No red portion had been visible; only blue.

When they had finished the task, the chaplain had presented the flag to Rachel saying *"This flag is offered by a grateful nation in memory of the faithful service performed by your loved one."*

The flag still sat in a wooden case in Patrick's office above his desk at home.

Weeks later, when Rachel had been ready to hear the details of the accident, one of the officers at Langley had explained to her that Patrick had indeed gone on a safe tour, just as she had been told by her husband prior to the trip. There had been no reason for him to have been threatened on this particular mission. They could not have predicted, however, that Patrick and Eric's lives would have been susceptible to danger as they had left the base that evening for an innocent dinner in town. Their flight had been scheduled to leave for home the following day. They had borrowed one of the cars from the base and had gone to a local bar and restaurant to celebrate their successful operation abroad. The small restaurant had been a safe one soldiers had frequented while overseas in Bahrain. Soldiers knew this particular establishment had good food, and the proprietor had welcomed their American dollars.

Rachel thought about the officer's detailed account of the accident itself.

Patrick was driving the car. The officers were headed to the restaurant, and they had not had anything to drink; they were sober. There was no indication of foul play on their part. It was 20:30 hours and it was dark. Three other officers were following them to the restaurant in another car. The three officers and two other witnesses on the scene said Patrick had been stopped at a traffic light, and when the light had changed to green, he had advanced into the intersection. At that time, a semi-truck carrying piping for a construction site nearby barreled through the red light at the crossroads and hit Patrick's car sideways on the driver's side. Two of the passengers were killed on impact. Patrick and Eric didn't feel any pain. Most likely they didn't know what had hit them. The car was dragged for several yards, and when released by the semi, it stood in the street right-side up. The reports say the driver of the semi had been drinking and had not adhered to the traffic signal. You have our full support if you elect to take legal action against the trucking company on Patrick and Eric's behalf, and we will assist with the investigation. Patrick's expertise in the surveillance field has been invaluable to the Air Force.

Rachel had listened to the military lawyer's proposal for litigation, but nothing had registered. Patrick had died. Money hadn't matter. As the weeks passed, however, Rachel remembered grasping the reality of her situation; she would need money to raise her sons. The Air Force had said they would support her and Dorothy if they had planned to pursue their case against the trucking company, and they had both decided to take them up on their offer of assistance.

Nearly two years later, after much paperwork and a multitude of court appearances, with delays from lawyers at home and abroad, both women won a large sum of money as a result of their patience. It would never suffice for the loss of her husband, Rachel remembered thinking, but the boys would have a roof over their heads, and they would be able to afford to go to college. Patrick would have wanted it that way.

Chapter 5

"AUNT ERIN!" THE boys squealed as they ran into her arms for a hug and then took off into the house to look for their cousin.

Erin started down the driveway to greet her sister-in-law.

Rachel slowly stretched her legs as she got out of the car. Five hours had turned into six when she had hit the city limits and rush-hour traffic, and now she was feeling the strain. Her head had been aching for about an hour, and she wondered how long it would take to be able to unwind. She had always begun her vacations with worries. Not that she *wanted* to begin them that way. But she was continually nagged by this relentless list of *gottas*; of obligations and insignificant chores back home that had to get done before she could enjoy her real vacation. She wished she could just tear that mental list up and say *to hell with all her responsibilities*!

Rachel realized momentarily that part of the tension she was feeling may have been due to delving so profoundly into her emotional past for those last few hours of the trip. She had resolved earlier in the drive to close the file of her former life the moment she got to New York, hadn't she? So as she stepped away from the car, she was resolute about stepping into a new life. She exhaled deeply and took in the fresh air around her.

"Finally, we're here!" Rachel said to Erin as she met her halfway up the driveway and gave her a big hug.

"Don't you have any baggage to bring in?" Erin asked as they turned to walk into the house.

"Not really. I packed this little bag for the three of us for tonight, since we're hitting the road again so early in the morning. I didn't want to have to lug in three big suitcases and then have to sit on them again to stuff everything back inside! Ski clothes take up so much room, don't they?"

They both laughed and locked arms as they walked inside the house.

"Okay, dinner is ready, and I'm almost packed. Kevin went out to the store to get a few items I forgot for the trip, but he just called and said he's on his way home. He wants to spend a little time with everyone before we leave tomorrow."

"Great! It really is too bad he has to work right up until the day before Christmas and can't go with us. I guess we can't all have teachers' schedules, right?"

Her sister-in-law was also a teacher; she taught social studies at a middle school nearby.

"Yep! But the trip will give us some girl-time to catch up on life, and time for the boys to get into some mischief," Erin responded as she took Rachel's coat and hung it in the closet in the foyer.

"I know, right? Brandon and Andrew can't stop talking about all the things they want to do there with Brad. They can't wait to take him on the toboggan slide."

"Okay, so tell me about this slide. Brad said the boys had mentioned it to him, but I didn't really understand what he was talking about. Isn't a toboggan some kind of carriage or something?"

"Noooo. It's a sleigh-type thing, but with sides on it," Rachel gestured, "and it fits from two to four people. It takes off from a thirty-foot-high ski jump, and you go down these chutes that end up on Mirror Lake for about one thousand feet."

"*On the lake?!*"

"Don't worry, its frozen! It's so much fun, Erin. I hadn't been to Lake Placid for years, so when we finally got there last year, I made sure we explored all the new things they have to offer, and we found the ski jump."

"And you're sure this toboggan-thing is safe?"

"Of course it is! Just wait. You'll love it. Oh, and you can also take a dog-sled ride around the lake for about ten to fifteen dollars. We did it last year, but I think I enjoyed it more than the boys did. They liked the thrill of the toboggan slide better."

"What about shopping?"

"Are you kidding?! Our lodge is right on the main street, so we'll be next to all the quaint little boutiques and shops. Now, you're just going to have to wait until we get there to hear about everything else. I'm not telling you anymore!"

Chapter 6

THE GOLDEN ARROW Lakeside Resort sat right in the middle of town at Lake Placid next to Mirror Lake. The interior of the lodge was decorated for the holidays with enormous fir trees adorned with colorful handmade ornaments and gold bows and tinsel. Miniature lights were scattered throughout the lobby illuminating the wooden beams in the ceiling. Rachel and Erin gazed at the garland and decorations as they walked over to the reception desk to check in.

As she waited at the counter, Rachel glanced down at a picture on the cover of their brochure and was reminded of her arrival with the boys the prior year at nightfall. There had been countless pine trees lining the streets of the village intertwined with twinkling fairy lights that had escorted them down the road to the lodge. She smiled as she recalled nearly hitting a pole as she had been distracted by the delicate luminaries glistening in the snow as she was approaching the lodge.

"May I have your name for the reservation?"

"Yes, Rachel Matthews."

"You have the Panther Suite for six reserved, correct?"

"Correct."

"And the ski package for Whiteface Mountain?"

"Yes."

"Okay, one moment while I process this," the receptionist said.

Rachel had reserved the Panther Suite way in advance. They had told her this week would be one of the busiest of the season, so she had booked it in December of the previous year. The suite had two cozy rooms; one with a king-sized bed, wood-burning fireplace, and walk-out balcony, and the other room with two queen-sized beds and a private veranda. She figured the boys would stay in the latter.

"Come on, Mom! Let's get this stuff in the room so we can go skiing!"

"Okay, hold your horses! We have to finish checking in, then unpack, then—"

"No unpacking, mom! We want to ski!"

"Okay, okay! We do have to go next-door to rent the skis, though."

Rachel hadn't wanted to buy the boys skis the previous year because at this age they were growing like weeds, and she had predicted that from one winter to the next, she'd have to replace the ski boots and the bindings for the skis all over again. And she had been right. They had both grown three inches in one year.

WHITEFACE MOUNTAIN HAD been the location of the Winter Olympic events twice; in 1932 and in 1980. From a distance, the mountain looked menacing for beginning skiers like Erin with its high vertical drop, but there were plenty of runs for beginning and intermediate skiers as well. Although Rachel was an advanced skier, as were her boys, she'd stay on the beginner slopes with Erin until she got comfortable enough to graduate to the intermediate slopes.

All five of them walked into the ski shop to rent their skis, and it became a game of choices. Do we get the longer skis or the shorter ones? The red poles or the blue ones? How should the boots feel? What about the helmet?

The technician at the shop was very helpful. He explained to Erin that she needed to get her boots before the skis. He asked for her shoe size, and when he brought her the appropriate boots, she laughed and said they looked like something an alien or an astronaut would wear. She took off her Uggs to try on the ski boots, and the technician told her she had too many layers of socks on.

"Oh yeah, I should have told you," Rachel concurred, "if you wear layered socks, it will just cut off your circulation or smash down the insulation of the socks. Socks need room to expand in order to keep the feet warm, so it's best to wear just one good pair."

"So which ones do you recommend?" Erin asked her.

"Hmm. I don't like either pair that you have on. I think you should just buy a pair of polypropylene socks. They'll whisk away the moisture from your feet. Here, I'll go get you a pair over by the counter."

After bringing Erin the new socks, the technician took over as Rachel sat on the bench to put on her own socks and boots. He explained to Erin that the boots needed to fit comfortably but snug from the calf to the toes. The heel shouldn't move when flexing the knee, but the toes should have a little wiggle room.

"It sounded so easy to just rent this stuff," Erin sighed.

"Okay," the technician said, "your foot shouldn't be moving around too much, because if the boot is too big, your feet will get cold. But your toes shouldn't be curling over either. They should come off the boot when you lean."

Erin stood up and leaned forward several times.

While the technician was taking care of Erin, Rachel went over to the skis to pick out a pair that fit her boots. She had brought her own boots on the trip, but she needed to rent the skis. The skis nowadays were so much better than they had been when she had been a skier in college, she reflected. Now they were shorter and had more surface area. She selected her skis, inserted the toes into the bindings, lined up the heels in the back, and snapped them on. *Perfect*, she thought. Now the poles.

As she wandered over to the wall where the red and blue poles were hanging so she could select the color that would match her height, she bumped right into another skier who had bent down unexpectedly in front of her to unbuckle his boots.

"*Oh shit!*" he exclaimed as he grabbed Rachel's arm to keep her from falling.

It was too late. Rachel found herself sitting on the floor at the feet of this tall athletic man in a space suit with gentle brown eyes and straight dark hair peeking out of his navy blue knit cap.

"Oh my goodness! I am so sorry! Here, please let me help you up," he said, extending both arms.

It was a little more difficult lifting her off the floor while in full ski garb than if she had been in her regular street clothes, so she was a little embarrassed.

"That's okay. I got it," she said.

"*Rachel?*"

"Do I know you?" she asked as she tried to compose herself.

"Rachel Hayes from Corcoran High School?"

Thomas J. Corcoran High School was the public school Rachel had attended in Syracuse near her parents' home when she was growing up. There had been about eighteen hundred students there at the time.

"Yes, it's Rachel."

Now that she was at eye level, she suddenly recognized him and she felt a pang of nervous excitement wash over her, not quite sure what to say next.

"I should know you, right?" she heard herself ask awkwardly.

"I hope so! You were on the Cougars basketball team for the girls, and I was a point guard on the guys' team. We went to the Prom together!"

"Michael Blanford?"

Of course it was. Why was she being so coy? *Get a grip.*

"One and the same! Gosh, it's been decades since I've seen you!" he said looking into her eyes as the memories flooded back from high school. "*Literally* decades!"

"Well don't make it sound as if we are *that* old!" she laughed.

Michael had been one of the biggest catches at Corcoran High back in the day. He had been attractive yet unassuming; he hadn't been aware of his appeal, even when the cheerleaders had yelled louder for him on the court than any other basketball player. She remembered him with his long black hair and those gorgeous soft eyes that sparkled when he smiled. He still looked like that now, she thought, only more mature and handsomely rugged.

Yep, she had just said 'handsomely rugged', hadn't she? Like a TV commercial, she mused.

Rachel had hung out with Michael for part of her senior year of high school, even though he had been a year younger and had been a junior. He had been in her advanced Spanish class that last year of school, and they had connected with a comfortable friendship. She remembered sitting next to him when they were in groups working on dialogues and skits to present in front of the class at the end of each unit. Vanessa, one of the girls in their group, had dubbed Michael *ratoncito*, or little mouse, because he had always been the shyest person in the group when having to get up in front of the class to recite a dialogue.

Since they had both played on the basketball teams, they had spent time together with other team members going to Lum's Burger Shop to eat after the games, to scary movies, or to play putt-putt golf. When the spring came along and it was time to look for Prom dates, the two had just assumed they'd go together as good friends. Rachel hadn't known then that Michael had harbored a secret crush on her. He may not have even known it himself until Prom night.

She recalled going to dinner with a group of friends to a nice restaurant in Syracuse prior to the Prom. Michael had grabbed her hand when leading her into the restaurant, and that's when she had felt the first tingle of infatuation. He had been the perfect gentleman when opening the door, pulling out her chair at the table, and pouring her water from the pitcher. He had flashed that big grin of his with those gorgeous straight teeth all night long. But Rachel also remembered thinking it had been too late for a crush, because she would be going off to college three months later and he would be staying back at Corcoran High for his senior year. She had decided not to get emotionally involved; best to continue being buddies.

As she was mentally ruminating through the pages of her high school years, she suddenly became aware of the familiar smell in front of her, bringing her back to the present. Could he still be wearing the same brand of cologne after all these years? *Old Spice?* She recollected the smell of the cologne that had attempted to seduce her when Michael had pulled her close to his chest during a dance at the Prom. At one point she had spilled some punch on her dress, and Michael had loaned her his handkerchief to wipe it off. She smiled as she remembered keeping the handkerchief and smelling the Old Spice on it for several days afterwards as it lay neatly folded in her bureau drawer. *Ah, those were the days...*

She blushed as the memory crept back of the last slow dance on Prom night. When the music had stopped at the end of the dance, Michael had pulled his face apart from hers and had softly kissed her on the lips. Then they had nervously stepped out of the dance and had looked around to see if anyone had caught sight of their exchange. It had probably been his first kiss, although it had not been hers. She had had a couple of boyfriends earlier in high school, but nothing serious; she wasn't even sure she could remember what their names had been. But all the memories about Michael and Prom night had come back to her as she stood there facing him in the ski shop after all these years.

Michael and Rachel suddenly realized they were standing in the middle of the shop staring at each other. She wondered if he was remembering Prom night as well.

"Rachel," Erin's voice came from around the corner, "I think I finally found the right boots and skis!"

"Great!" she responded, turning to look at her sister-in-law.

"Oh, am I interrupting something?" Erin asked as she looked back and forth between her flustered sister-in-law and this gorgeous man from who knows where.

"No, of course not!" Rachel replied rather quickly. "Erin, this is an old friend of mine from high school, believe it or not. Michael, meet Erin Hayes, and Erin, this is Michael Blanford."

Michael extended his hand to Erin as she clumsily shifted her ski poles from her right hand to the left and ended up dropping the poles on the floor.

"Allow me," Michael said picking them up quickly and handing them to Erin.

"Are you sisters?" he asked Rachel.

"No, Erin is married to my brother. You probably didn't know Kevin because he was about three years ahead of me in high school."

There was an awkward silence again as the three of them stood there. Then the boys came up from behind and started handing things to their moms.

"Wow," Michael said with a big smile. "Three sons?"

"No," Rachel laughed. "Two are mine, and one is Erin's." She quickly introduced them to him.

"Do you have any children?" Rachel asked.

"I have one daughter. She's seventeen going on thirty," he said rolling his eyes.

They all laughed.

"Well," he said, "looks like you need to get that equipment rented so the boys can hit the slopes. And I need to pick up my skis. I'm having them waxed here. But maybe I'll see you all on the slopes."

"I seriously doubt it," Erin responded. "I'm a beginner. I mean a *real* beginner!"

Michael shook hands with everyone again and Rachel and Erin went over to the counter to fill out their contracts for the rentals. Rachel felt as if a page had been ripped out of the journal on her fresh new life and had been torn into small pieces. If she was going create this new life for herself, wasn't she supposed to be collecting new exciting experiences to record in her journal instead of shredding every page as it was being written?

"Crap," she said to Erin as they waited in line away from the boys' earshot. "He was such a catch in high school. Wasn't he gorgeous?! I should have asked if he wanted to catch up later for coffee or something. No, wait, that's the guy's job. He's probably married anyway. I mean, he said he has a daughter."

"He's not married, Rachel."

"How do you know? Did he say something to you?"

"No," Erin smiled. "I saw him look at your ring finger when he picked up the ski poles for me."

"You're crazy! So how does that translate into him not being married?"

"Well, my dear, a man doesn't look at a woman's ring finger if he isn't available."

"Really?"

"Really. I know."

"I'm not going to ask you how you know. Okay, so why didn't he stick around or ask to see me later or something?"

"Because the boys walked up to us at that point. I think that may have confused him and he wasn't quite sure whether or not you were single."

"But I *am*! Shoot. I couldn't have very well just blurted out that I'm single, right?"

"Don't worry, he didn't see a husband, so if he's interested, he'll find you."

"Like how? There are eighty-six ski runs out on that mountain!"

Rachel was up next. She filled out the rental forms and charged the fees to her credit account. As Erin filled out her forms, Rachel walked over towards the doors to find the boys so she could tell them their ski equipment was ready.

"Rachel," she heard Michael's voice again. "Are you staying here at Lake Placid?"

"Yes!"

Oh my God, I can't believe he came back.

"Where?" he asked.

"The lodge next door. What about you?"

Just makin' conversation, she said to herself. *I'm as cool as a cucumber.*

"I'm staying at a cottage right outside of town with some friends."

"Oh," she said.

Quick, what do I say now?

He turned to walk towards the door. She wanted to pull

him back.

"So," he said, "I'd love to catch up with you and hear about what you've been doing all these years since high school."

"Yes, that would be nice!"

Did that sound too anxious?

"Okay, well, my buddies and I come into town every night to eat dinner, and I hear your lodge has a great lounge. Do you want to meet me there for a drink before dinner tonight? Or after dinner?"

"Sure! Can we try after dinner? I'm just not sure what time we'll have our act together for dinner."

"Sure. And bring your husband, too."

"No husband," she blurted out. "What time?"

"We can play it by ear. We'll probably be there around eight. But no rush; just show up whenever you're ready."

"Okay!"

I'll make sure it's okay, she said to herself, excited about someone for the first time since she had met Patrick.

Patrick. Oh dear. Patrick, is this okay? Can you send me a sign to let me know if it is okay? Like maybe causing me to fall on the slopes so I can't make it tonight? No, no, not that. But maybe they'll close the lounge for some reason, or maybe Michael will be waylaid by his friends. Aghhh! I just hope it is okay! Please send me a sign!

Rachel exited the door and stood outside the ski shop with clenched fists jumping up and down in the snow.

"Mom, are you okay?"

"Oh. Oh, yes, I'm fine. Just excited about skiing, sweetie. Here, let's get these skis on."

Erin came up behind her. "I saw that."

"What?"

"The jumping up and down. He came back, didn't he?"

"Was it that obvious?"

"Nah, I saw him when he walked back," she said pointing over to the door.

Rachel pushed her sister-in-law and nearly knocked her over.

"Hey! I don't know how to walk in these space boots yet, remember?!"

They both laughed.

Chapter 7

THE KIDS HAD an ideal day of skiing. All the slopes on Whiteface Mountain had been groomed and were in great condition. Rachel spent most of the time on the easiest slopes with Erin and Brad, while Andrew and Brandon ventured off on their own to the intermediate slopes. She had prohibited them from skiing any advanced slopes for the first two days.

"So which run did you like the best, Aunt Erin? Fox, Deer or Bear run?" Brandon asked at the dinner table that evening.

"I have no idea!" she responded. "I was so nervous that I just kept my eyes focused on going down! I have no clue what the scenery looked like around me!"

"You'll get the feel of it," Rachel responded. "Tomorrow should be more fun!"

"If I can walk! Gosh my legs hurt so much! Isn't anyone else feeling what I feel?"

They all laughed.

"Now, I don't expect you to stay with me all day tomorrow, Rachel. I think I can find my way back to the bunny slopes and practice on my own. I'll have Brad with me for part of the day, too. Then in the afternoon he may be ready to try an easy intermediate slope with his cousins. *Easy* is the key word here, boys."

"Don't worry, I'll stick with you all day, mom," Brad responded. "I could use some more practice."

"Well, we don't have to plan," Rachel said, "let's just see how it goes. It's only going to be our second day on skis, and we have four more days to go."

As group continued their chatter, Rachel noticed Andrew was quiet. She leaned over to him and whispered, "Are you okay, sweetie?"

"Yeah, mom. I guess I did get that cold afterwards, but I don't want to ruin this vacation for anyone."

"Maybe you need to take tomorrow off and just sleep. We have plenty of days here," she said brushing the hair out of his eyes and feeling his forehead for a temperature. "I think I'm going to have the resort's doctor check you out."

"Aw, mom! I don't need a doctor!"

"Well, just a quick check. I'll see if I can get someone here after dinner."

"But we were going to go to the indoor pool," he pleaded.

"You can still go. Just tell the boys you'll meet them there. I have to meet some friends down in the lounge later on, but I'll get Aunt Erin to stay with you while the doctor is here. Then you can go to the pool if nothing is wrong. I promise."

He gave her a look.

"I promise! Unless you do have a virus or something that you could be passing around to other people. In that case you'll need to take 24 hours off with an antibiotic. Deal?"

"Okay," he answered with his head hung low on his chest.

"It'll be okay. The worst case scenario: you have to stay in bed for a day. The best case scenario: you go to the pool a little late but you meet a gorgeous little blonde girl your age on the way there."

"Mom!"

AFTER DINNER, RACHEL called the resort's medical clinic, and they said they would send someone within the half hour. Erin urged her sister-in-law to go and meet Michael downstairs in the lounge by telling her she would stay with Andrew in the room waiting for the doctor. She promised to call her on the cell phone to let her know what the doctor said.

The boys had run upstairs to get into their swim suits after they had left the table, and Rachel had ventured down to the lounge. It was 8:30. She stopped at the ladies room on her way to check her teeth for food bits, and to apply a little bit of lipstick. *Not too much*, she thought to herself, because she didn't want it to look as if she were getting all fancy for him. Maybe she should comb her hair a little while she was at it. *Oh what the hell*, she thought, as she wiped off the lipstick with a tissue and threw it in the trash.

She felt nervous entering the lounge on her own. Michael's buddies would surely be standing around him, and she would look as if she were picking him up at the bar. Well, she *was*, wasn't she?

Michael saw Rachel before she saw him. "Hi, Rach! Over here!"

He walked towards her, and when he reached her, he bent down and lightly kissed her on the cheek. She thought she was going to pass out.

Smile, she told herself, *smile like you do this every day.*

"Hi, Mike," she responded. "Wow, this is a nice lounge!"

How stupid. You just let on that you've never been here before. Well, it's true, isn't it?

"Yeah, it is! This is my first time here, but my buddies have talked about it."

Whew.

"So let me introduce you to a few of the guys, and then I want to hear what you've been up to all these years."

He took her hand and led her over to the bar where four of his friends were drinking beer while boasting and joking about their escapades from the day of skiing. After introducing her to his friends, he called the bartender over to order her a drink.

"So what are you drinking?" Michael asked.

"Chardonnay, please."

"Citrus or caramel?"

"Oaky," she responded, impressed with his question.

"What kind of oaked to you have back there?" he asked the bartender.

"Cakebread Cellars and Du Mol."

"Okay, I'll take two of the Du Mol."

Expensive, she thought.

"I don't know too many men who are chardonnay drinkers," she heard herself say, wondering if she had just insulted him.

"I appreciate a good glass of wine. I live in California near the Russian River, and I guess I've become a little spoiled with my wines. I've actually been tinkering with the idea of owning a winery someday."

"Oh, tell me about it!" she said earnestly interested.

"Nope! Ladies first. Start from the beginning. I want to know all about what happened when you went off to college, what you majored in, where you went from there, and about your kids; all of it."

She noticed he hadn't asked about her husband; just the kids.

"Do you promise to take a turn?" she asked.

"Yes, I promise," he laughed. "But it'll take a long time, so we may have to meet back here again tomorrow," he said with a smile.

Okay with me! Surely he couldn't be married, or he wouldn't be asking me for another date. Is this really a date? No, not a date. Just talking; that's all this is.

"Come on, let's go over to a table," he said, while picking up the two glasses of wine from the bar and walking with her to a small cozy table by the fireplace.

"Now, start from the beginning. You went to college at the University of Virginia, and I remember we wrote each other a few letters your first semester there. I recall seeing you briefly in Syracuse at Thanksgiving and Christmas that year, but then I lost track of you."

Rachel told Michael her story. She started with her college experience, and then she talked about meeting Patrick, getting married, and having Brandon and Andrew. She finally got around to telling him about Patrick's job and how it led to his last trip abroad and his accidental death.

"I'm so sorry, Rachel."

"It's okay. I mean, it's been three years, so we're all making do. The boys are super busy with school and activities and I am busy with work. I'm a teacher, you know."

It had been over an hour since they had been talking, and Rachel had completely forgotten to check her cell phone for messages from Erin.

"Mike, I just need to check my phone for a minute. I'm not trying to be rude," she smiled. "Andrew was looking a little feverish this evening, so I had Erin call the resort's medic to check in on him."

"Sure! I'll go over and order us another glass of wine while you make your call."

Rachel checked her phone and saw the text message: *Andrew okay. Just needs rest. A little fever. Gave him Tylenol.*

Rachel decided to call Erin even though the message had been clear.

"Hey, I'm just touching base. Got your message."

"Everyone is fine here! Not to worry. The boys are headed back from the pool now, and we're getting ready to rent a movie on TV. How about you? Things going well for you?"

"Yes," she sighed. "Erin, I could really like Michael a lot. I know it's only been one day, but he is so genuine. He's polite, respectful, a good listener, funny; everything."

"So? What is your hesitation?"

"He lives in California."

"Hmm. Well, you never know."

"*California*, Erin."

"Just try to enjoy yourself, Rachel. You have to live in the moment. At least you know up front what you are getting into."

"I'm not getting into anything!"

"You know what I mean! Rachel, just let yourself have some fun. Remember what you told me Darlene said to you? About opening up your heart?"

"No opening, Erin. Not ready."

"Yes you are. And we're not talking about a serious thing here, Rach. He does live in California, okay? So stop over-thinking this. Just have fun. Sleep with him if he asks."

"Erin! I can't believe you said that!" she laughed.

"Join the twenty-first century, dear! Dating is a lot different than it was all those years ago when you met Patrick."

"Okay," she whispered quickly into her phone, "he's coming back to the table. Gotta go."

"Sleep tight!" Erin said.

"You are so bad! Bye!"

"Everything okay?" he asked while placing the two glasses of wine on the table.

"More than okay."

Did I just say that? Whatever. Erin said I have to live in the moment. I don't care what he reads into it.

"So do I get to hear a little bit about you now?" Rachel asked as she took a sip of her wine.

"What do you want to know?" he asked looking into her eyes as they melted into his.

"Oh, okay," she said timidly. "You want questions. I heard you went to California to study after graduating from

Corcoran High, right?"

"Yes. Stanford."

"Wow! What did you study?"

"Pre-law. It's a long story, but I'll try to make it short. My first two years there, I messed up and almost dropped out. I got caught up with some guys who were into drugs, and I became a lost soul until I discovered the law."

"Drugs?"

"Marijuana; nothing else. I hung out with a crowd that did more partying than studying. They were all flying on their dad's coat tails, like I was. You know, parents who had money and paid for whatever you wanted. I had a fast car and I thought I was invincible."

"I can't picture that, because you were so shy in high school."

"Late bloomer!" he laughed. "Anyway, one day I had too much to drink and hadn't slept much, so I ended up falling asleep at the wheel and veering off the road to hit a tree. I wound up in the hospital. I had been alone in the car, so no one got hurt but myself. It was the wake-up call I needed, though. I was lucky to have just broken a leg."

"Wow. That *was* lucky."

"Yep. While recovering in the hospital, and later at my apartment, I had plenty of time to reflect on my life and goals. The professors at Stanford were fabulous; they sent over a ton of work for me to do so I could recover my credits. It was then that my advisor paid me a visit and got me hooked on the thought of studying law."

"So you are a lawyer?" she asked surprised.

"Yes. Most people in the Silicon Valley area go into technology, but Stanford has a reputable law school, so I continued my studies there."

"What kind of law?"

"Well, at first I had thought about following the path of William Rehnquist. As an alumnus of Stanford, he had come back to talk to our graduating class, and I was awestruck by his credentials and accomplishments.

"The former Supreme Court Justice?"

"Yes. But while I was pursuing my traditional JD," he stopped for a moment, "wait, am I getting too technical here?"

"No, I get it. Your *Juris Doctor*, right?"

"Right. How do you know so much?"

"I just read! Okay, back to your story."

"Not boring you?" he asked sincerely.

"Not boring me." *Not at all*, she thought.

"Okay, so while I was pursuing my JD, I became interested in environmental law. I started to customize my degree, and in my third year of law school, I began helping real clients with real issues in what they called *clinics* at Stanford."

"Got it. Clinics."

"I graduated and then struggled like most young lawyers who join firms and work twenty-four-seven for crumbs while dreaming about the one big case that would make them rich. It was rough. I told my dad to stay out of the picture; I had to do it on my own. Anyway, one day I was asked to assist with a case in which the client had remembered me from the clinics I had worked in at Stanford. Apparently he had been impressed with my work at the time, and when he found out I was on the staff at the firm, he told them he would deal only with me. I couldn't believe my luck. It was a big case with big bucks attached."

"Did you win?"

"I won," he smiled with sincere humility.

"Big bucks?"

"Yes," he laughed, "big bucks. So I used the money to go out on my own."

"You have your own law firm?" she asked.

"Yes. It's a small one, but we're effective and have built a strong reputation. We work mostly with environmental policy, even though we've been expanding for the past five years into other areas."

"I'm so impressed, Mike."

"Don't be. It's just me. Still the same old Mike. And now I feel like I've monopolized the conversation!"

"Wait, one more question," she said. "You told us at the ski rental you have a daughter. Are you still married?"

Please say no. Please say no.

"No. That's a whole other story."

"I have time!

"Really?"

"Really. I told you my story, so I want to hear all about yours."

"Well, when I was nineteen and kind of lost in undergrad, I met a girl I fell hard for. She was a hippy-type, and she was part of the partying group I mentioned. We dated for about a year, and then she got pregnant. Only I never knew about it. She broke up with me and I was devastated. That's when I hit bottom and ended up in the hospital. When I got out of the hospital, she was gone. There was a note on my bureau at the apartment saying she had moved back home."

"So she went back home to have the baby?"

"Yes, thank God. I am so happy she didn't have an abortion, because I can't imagine my life without Ellie."

"Ellie is your daughter?"

"Yes. And she's been the love of my life."

"So how did you find out about her? I mean, what happened?"

"Okay, so now I *know* I've dominated the conversation! If you want to hear part two, you'll have to meet me again tomorrow."

"Okay, but just one more question."

"Nope! Questions are for tomorrow. Come on, I've heard they have a nice dancing place here somewhere. I think they call it Roomers Night Club, and it's open until 3."

"Three in the morning?!"

"Come on, lady, you aren't that old! Just one year older than me."

"You brat! You're on! I'll show you I can stay awake longer than you!" she laughed.

They found Roomers and were surprised to see how crowded it had become at ten o'clock at night. It was *oldies* night, and Rachel immediately recognized the song they were playing by Three Dog Night.

Mike grasped Rachel's hand and walked her over to the bar to take a seat.

"One more chardonnay? I'm having a hard time letting you go," he said.

"Sure. I'm not driving."

God, that was insensitive, she told herself, *just after he shared about the driving accident that left him wrapped around a tree.*

Michael smiled and ordered the wine.

"So," he said, "how about some pancakes tomorrow morning?"

"Pancakes?" she asked confused.

"Yeah. The restaurant at this lodge has pancakes with the best maple syrup produced in the Adirondacks. Did you know New York is the second largest producer of maple syrup in the United States?"

"Really?"

"Yes ma'am! Oh, and they make a fabulous maple wrap here that is to die for."

"Maple wrap?"

"Scrambled eggs, cheddar, ham, and maple syrup wrapped in a grilled flour tortilla."

"You sound like a commercial! How do you know all that? I thought this was your first time at this lodge."

"Actually, this was my first time at the *lounge,* where we met tonight. But I've been coming to this lodge since I was a child. My family and I used to ski here every winter during the holidays, so I got to know the cook quite well. Hence the maple wrap."

"Is it the same cook they have now?"

"Same one," he said. "I'll introduce you to her tomorrow morning at breakfast."

I guess this means I'm meeting him for breakfast, she thought. *Or does it mean I'm supposed to wake up in his bed and go to breakfast with him? I can't believe I'm even considering the idea!*

"Listen," he said, "do you hear that? They're playing our song. Want to dance?"

"Sure."

Michael led her onto the dance floor and took her right hand in his as he put his other arm around her waist; just like in high school. He pulled her close.

"Do you remember this song? *Cherish*?"

"I do," she answered truthfully. "But I don't remember who sang it."

He had bent down to hear her answer over the music, and his ear had brushed her lips. She felt a quiver run through her. She could smell the Old Spice on his neck and it brought back a comfortable memory. She was nervous, and she wondered if he felt the same way.

"The Association."

"What?" she asked.

"The Association wrote this song. Do you remember Prom night at Corcoran High?"

"Yes. I asked you to the Prom in my senior year. It really was a wonderful night, Mike. You were such a gentleman, and I had so much fun." She smiled at the memory.

He smiled back and bent down again to talk into her ear. "This was the last song they played that night; our last dance."

"Really?"

"Yes. It was the number one song on the charts back when the Association released it in 1966, but it was still popular years later, and I guess it still is!"

The song transported her back to her Prom night. She recalled having hoped this other guy in her science class would ask her to the Prom, but he never did, so she had asked Michael to go with her. She had suspected Michael had a secret crush on her, so she presumed he'd say yes to her request, and he did. She hadn't meant to take advantage of his feelings; she had just wanted to be with someone with whom she knew she'd have a nice time.

Michael pulled her closer and rested her hand on his shoulder as he put both arms around her waist. She turned her head inward and rested it on his chest as he sang along to the lyrics of the song. At that moment, she felt as if she belonged there; she felt safe.

Cherish is the word I used to describe
All the feeling that I have hiding here for you inside
You don't know how many times I've wished that I had told you
You don't know how many times I've wished that I could hold you
You don't know how many times I've wished that I could mold you
Into someone who could cherish me as much as I cher-
ish you
And I do cherish you

It seemed as if the song had lasted at least twenty minutes instead of five. Michael pulled slightly away but continued holding onto Rachel's waist. She looked up at him and saw tenderness in his eyes as he looked back. He lowered his head and kissed her lips lightly. He barely pulled away, just enough to look into her eyes again, as if searching for something.

Rachel understood what he was looking for. After the last dance on Prom night, Michael had kissed her in the same manner; just a gentle kiss on the lips. But the responsiveness he had been seeking had not been reciprocated. So he had pulled away, and had continued the evening laughing and partying with their friends with no expectation for an impending romance.

But tonight was different. They were all grown up now.

This time Michael didn't wait for the silent answers he sought from her eyes. He pulled her close to his chest and kissed her passionately as he held her in his arms. She kissed him back, and she could feel the blood running into her heart and resounding loudly in her ears. He held her face in one of his hands and pulled away slightly. He rested his forehead on hers and looked down at her. She wondered if he could feel her heavy breathing and her heart leaping out of her skin. He smiled and kissed her again, but this time lightly on the forehead.

"Come on, I want to take you somewhere."

Is he taking me to his cottage? Is this it? Am I actually doing this? I don't think I'm ready! But I don't want him to dump me because I'm being so indecisive, either!

He led her off the dance floor and held onto her waist from behind as they exited the night club.

"I'm taking you to the moon."

"The moon?" she asked confused.

"You'll see!"

He grabbed her hand and they headed to the elevators in the lobby. They got off on the third floor, went to the end of the hall, and opened a door that said *Employees Only*. They entered the small space and it was full of cleaning supplies, brooms, mops, and a large container in the corner overflowing with dirty towels.

"Are we allowed to be in here?" she whispered.

"*I* am," he grinned mysteriously. "Okay, now over here by this broom closet is a low entryway you have to duck into, so you need to keep your head down when you go through it."

"Where does it go?"

"It leads to a dormer. It's part of the structure of this building that protrudes from the roof. What's unique about this particular dormer is that it has an opening leading out onto a balcony. The other dormer passages end with a window or a skylight. I discovered this one as a child when I used to come here for the holidays with my family."

"How on earth did you find it?"

"That's another story."

"I know; I'll have to wait for breakfast to hear more stories."

He laughed. "Okay, trust me?" he asked.

She nodded yes.

"All right, I'll go first."

He entered the passageway and motioned for her to follow. She bent low and walked through the entrance. It was about four feet high and quite narrow.

"Remember, keep your head down."

A moment later she heard him say "Ouch!"

"I thought you said we needed to keep our heads down low!"

"Okay, so I'm a little taller than you!" he laughed.

Michael was probably about six foot three, and she was five foot eight.

Rachel saw the light of the moon and stars as she neared the end of the narrow passageway. She walked out onto the miniature balcony and gazed into the most beautiful night sky she had ever seen. It took her breath away. Michael stood behind her, giving her the full view of the indescribable scene below them. Neither one said a word. It was beyond vocabulary.

They gazed down at the Lake Placid village. It was surrounded by rows of pine trees leading to the glassy lake beyond, and their twinkling lights reflected like tiny diamonds in the moonlight. Michael sensed the cold and he took off his jacket and put it around Rachel's shoulders. He enveloped her in his arms from behind and pulled her close to him. She never felt the cold.

"My father died when I was sixteen. I don't know if you knew that," he said.

"No, I didn't!" she pulled slightly away and turned around to look into his eyes.

"It's okay," he said kissing her on the top of her head and pulling her back into the warmth of his arms. "He died in October that year. We had already booked this ski trip way in advance, so my mom decided to keep the trip. That's the year my sister and I found this passageway. The grown-ups had gone out somewhere after dinner one evening, and the cook brought us here after her dinner shift was over."

"The cook you're going to introduce to me tomorrow at breakfast?"

"Yes," he smiled, "that's the one. Her name is really Miss Frieda, but we call her *Cook*. She knew my family from all the Christmas vacations we spent here. My dad had always made a big deal about her cooking, and my mom adored her. She once helped Cook by giving her some money to put her son through college. Cook was pretty upset when mom told her about dad's death, because they were like family."

"So she showed you this secret place?"

"Yes. One evening she had asked Elaine and me to stay after dinner for a special dessert she had concocted for us. Elaine is my older sister, by the way. I'm not sure if you knew her."

"No."

"Anyway, I think Cook sensed our sadness, and she wanted to give us a special gift; something money couldn't buy. So she brought us the dessert and showed us this secret passage. She made us swear to never reveal this little gem to anyone; it would be ours and ours alone. Elaine and I made a pact; we promised each other that one of us would try to come here every year at Christmas to say a little prayer for dad."

Michael fell silent for a few moments. Rachel didn't want to pierce the silence with words. She knew he was probably keeping his promise to his sister to say the prayer for his dad. Little did she know he was actually thanking his father for bringing Rachel to this place at the same time as he was here.

"Elaine and I came to Lake Placid for the holidays with mom for about six more years, but after college, we started going our separate ways. I had moved to California, so it wasn't always possible to get here. Sometimes Elaine gets back here and writes to tell me about it, and sometimes I come here with Ellie or on my own."

"Thank you for sharing this, Mike. I know it's very special to you."

"It is," he said looking down at her and smiling. "I've never brought anyone else here before tonight. Except Ellie, of course."

He gently cupped her chin with his warm hand, pulled her face up to his, and kissed her for a long time. Everything around them disappeared into the night as they explored each other's passion.

Chapter 8

"WHAT TIME DID you get in last night?" Erin asked Rachel as she lifted her head off the pillow at seven o'clock the next morning.

"Late! I think it was around midnight," she answered.

"Tell me! You have to tell me!" Erin insisted.

"I am so confused, Erin."

"That's not the answer I had expected. I thought you'd tell me you had a night of frolicking or something."

"Not quite. It was gentle and tender and wonderful."

"So you *did* sleep with him."

"No, I did *not*!" she answered defensively. "We just danced and talked and then visited the moon."

"Okay, I'm not going to ask you to explain that. But what are you confused about?" she asked as she threw on her bathrobe and turned on the coffeepot in their suite.

"I think I'm falling in love."

"Holy crap, Rach! He lives in *California*!"

"Exactly."

"Okay, now I see why you are confused."

She sat on the bed next to Rachel. "So what are you going to do?

"I have no idea. I'm trying to do what you told me, you know, just have fun and see where it takes me. But if it takes me to California…"

"Yeah, I know."

"I can't go to California, Erin. My folks and you guys are here in New York, and the boys and I have our lives in Virginia. And my job. And Patrick's parents." She sighed heavily and folded her arms around her knees as she sat on her bed.

"Well, don't get ahead of yourself. You said it yourself: take this one day at a time. This might just be a holiday romance. At least it is opening the way to looking at life and love without Patrick, you know?"

"Yeah, I suppose so. What time is it, anyway?"

"About seven fifteen. Why?"

"I'm supposed to meet Michael at eight for breakfast. So I guess I'd better get in the shower. What time did you all go to bed last night?"

"We stayed up until the movie ended; around eleven thirty. I'm surprised I didn't hear you come in, but I guess I was dead to the world after all that skiing yesterday."

"Oh yeah, how do your ski-legs feel this morning?"

"Better! And I'm ready for another day of punishment!" she laughed. "Okay, so you go get your shower first. I'm going to let the boys sleep in a little more, and we'll all meet you downstairs probably by the time you're done having breakfast with Michael."

"Okay, thanks. Really. I don't want you to think I'm putting this all on you. I'll meet up with you guys downstairs and then we can go skiing. I want to ski with you again today, okay?"

"What about Michael?"

"I think he's going skiing with his buddies, but I'll find out more at breakfast."

BREAKFAST WAS INDEED a treat, just as Michael had described it. He had met her in the Generations Restaurant and they had eaten more than their share of the maple wraps.

"Rachel, I'm going to be skiing with Ian and Daniel this morning, but what do you think about you and the boys meeting me midpoint up the mountain for lunch in the restaurant? You know where I'm talking about, right?"

"Boule's Bistro? The one on Boreen run?"

The Bistro was one of six restaurants on the mountain where skiers could go for a bite to eat during the day and not have to take off all their ski gear to do so; except their skis, or course. The Bistro would be perfect, because it was midway up the mountain and it intersected with Boreen run, one of the beginner runs, so Erin and Brad would be able to get off at the lift and then ski down easily from there.

"Yeah, that's the one," he said.

"Sure, I think that would be fine." She sounded a bit hesitant.

"Hey, if you don't think the boys should meet me, I'll understand."

"No, it's okay. But no holding hands or anything."

"Promise! I'll be on my best behavior!" he said reaching across the table and giving her a peck on the lips.

"Now you see?! You can't do that!" she laughed.

"I know! I'm just getting my kisses in now since I have to behave later!"

AFTER BREAKFAST RACHEL met up with Erin and the boys and they set off for a day of skiing on soft powdered snow that had been blown the night before to get ready for the skiers in the morning. Rachel and Erin started out on the beginner slopes until Erin felt a little more relaxed with her turns and stops. Eventually the moms joined their sons on the intermediate slopes, and this time Erin felt comfortable enough to watch some of the scenery as she snowploughed her way down the mountain. She skied slowly and sensibly and had a better time than the previous day.

By noon they were ravenous and set off for the open lodge at midpoint on the slopes. They propped up their skis and poles outside, and locked up whatever else in lockers.

Rachel didn't see Michael anywhere. It was a large place, and she didn't want to look too obvious to the boys while she searched for him. She wanted it to appear as if she were running into an old friend by chance. She had no idea how they would take this.

"Hey, is that you, Rachel?" she heard him ask.

She swiftly turned around to see Michael standing behind her with a tray of food.

Was that too obvious?

"Michael Blanford?" she asked.

"Yeah, I saw you in the ski rental shop yesterday, remember?" he responded. "Old classmate from high school?"

Good job, Mike; keep it going. Hopefully the boys are

buying this.

"Sure, I remember!" she said. "Erin and boys, this is Michael Blanford from my high school days."

"He already said that, mom," Andrew responded as Rachel turned beet red in the face.

They all went in different directions to get their food at the counters and then came back to the wooden picnic table to eat. While the boys were gone, Michael had grabbed her hand under the table.

"Mike! You promised!"

"I can't help myself," he said laughing. "Don't worry, mom, I checked to make sure the boys were way over by the counter getting their burgers. Rach, really, I'm not going to do anything that will hurt you or the boys. I get it."

No sooner than he had said that, Andrew and Brandon came back to the table and plunked down in their gear to devour their burgers and fries.

"Hey," Brandon asked Michael. "What did you ski today?"

Michael went into some animated stories about the slopes he had skied and the funny and dangerous encounters he had had with his buddies as they navigated their way down the double-diamond slopes. Maybe he exaggerated a bit.

"Wow!" Andrew said. "Can we go with you after lunch?!"

Oh-oh.

"Guys, I thought you were going to ski with Brad all day today," Rachel said.

"Oh, yeah. Yeah. How about tomorrow, Mike?" Andrew said.

They were already calling him Mike.

"Well, let's see what your mom says tomorrow," Michael responded.

Brad chimed in. "You guys go ahead today! I want to ski with my mom a little bit. I'm going to show her what I learned."

"Yeah," Erin said, "you guys go ahead. And Rachel, you go too. Brad and I will do some skiing together and we'll catch up with you later."

"Mom, *please?*" the boys implored. Brandon stuck his lower lip out and cocked his head like a puppy. Andrew looked at him and followed suit.

Twins; they always stick together!

"Argh! Okay, okay!" she responded to their pleas. "But we have to start with the *safest* black diamond slope on this side of the mountain, okay?"

"Yaaayyyy!!!" the boys responded. "Let's go, Mike!"

"Whoa! We're not even done with lunch!" Rachel said. "Let's finish here, everyone hit the bathroom, and then we can go. It's important to rest every now and then so you don't get overly tired and take any crazy risks."

"Okey-dokey," Brandon answered.

Rachel and Michael snuck a clandestine look at each other and smiled as they looked down at the food in front of them. She kept thinking about the kisses the night before. She had been thinking about them all morning as she skied, but now she'd have to put those thoughts aside as she took on the challenges of the black diamonds.

EVERYONE HAD SKIED to their heart's content and they were exhausted by five o'clock. Best to quit when your body tells you it has had enough for the day. Michael had left Rachel and the boys at the intermediate slopes around four o'clock where they had joined Erin and Brad to ski for another hour. He had headed down to the lodge for a beer with his friends, and back to his cottage for a shower and some dinner in town.

Rachel and Erin had gone with the boys to the indoor pool for an hour before getting ready for dinner. Then they all took turns showering and watching TV, piling a mess of wet towels and dirty clothes on the floor, and leaving opened bags of chips and half-full cans of soda strategically placed around the room.

After dinner, they went back to their rooms for coats and boots and headed outside to walk around in the village and do some shopping.

Brandon had been dating some little girl in middle school, if you could call it dating, and had wanted to shop for a stuffed animal to take back to her when they returned to Virginia. Andrew and Brad would never get the chance to tease him about it, though, because he and his mom had secretly conspired to hide the gift before the boys could ask who it was for. Rachel was glad her sons both trusted her to keep a confidence.

An hour had passed, and Erin noticed Rachel looking around as they walked through the town, as if looking for someone.

"Is his cottage somewhere here in town, Rach?

"Whose cottage?" she asked her sister-in-law.

"Oh, come on, you know whose!" Erin laughed and

locked arms with her as they walked along the brightly lit shops.

"Look, why don't you call him," she continued. "Do you have his cell phone number?"

"Who do you think I am?" she responded feigning innocence.

Erin gave her a look.

"Okay," Rachel said as she looked away and smiled, "I have his phone number. He wrote it on a napkin and gave it to me at breakfast this morning in case we couldn't find each other at lunch today on the mountain."

"Okay, so call him!" Erin said hitting her sister-in-law on the arm.

"I don't have my cell phone with me. And even if I did, what would I say? Come out and play with us?"

"I have my cell phone, smarty-pants. So call him," Erin responded pushing the phone into her hands.

"I'm serious. What do I say?"

"Well, how about you invite him to meet us and we all go on the toboggan ride you told us about? Isn't it near here?"

"Yeah, but—"

"Rachel, call him! You know you want to see him, so stop over-thinking everything."

"But what about the boys? They'll figure it out for sure this time!"

"Oh who cares? They'll just think their mom has a friend. Call."

"Okay, okay. I'll call when the boys are busy in a shop or something."

"I have an idea," Erin said. "We just passed a candy

shop that way," she pointed to three shops behind them.

"Are you trying to fatten up my boys?" she laughed.

The boys were happy about the prospect of going to the candy store and spending the money their moms had just given them for some treats.

"Oh, and can you get me some M&M's, Andrew?" Rachel asked fidgeting in her pocket for some extra cash.

"Sure, mom!"

Erin stayed outside with Rachel as she dialed the number Michael had given her.

"He won't answer Erin, I just know it."

"Hello?"

It was him on the other line!

"Say something!" Erin whispered.

"Hi, Mike. It's Rachel."

"I know. What's up?"

"How did you know it was me?"

"Because I was hoping you would call, and I didn't recognize this number."

"It's Erin's phone. Anyway, do you know if the toboggan ride is open in the evenings?"

"Yep. That's when it is the most fun! They light up the ramp along the way, and the whole lake lights up as well when the inner tube shoots out onto it."

"Wanna go? I was thinking of taking the boys."

"Yeah I wanna go! When? Now?"

He sounded anxious to see her; exactly what Rachel had been hoping.

"Yes," she responded, as if he had just proposed to her.

"Okay, are you in town?"

"Yeah. We're at the candy shop." She cringed as she

said it.

"Okay, pick me up some M&Ms and I'll meet you at the ride in twenty minutes."

"Really?" she asked, as if surprised he had accepted.

"Really. Go get me some M&Ms," he said hanging up the phone.

She smiled as big as her mouth could smile without cracking her lips wide open, and then she grabbed Erin and hugged her in a bear hug.

"What's up, mom?" Brandon asked coming out of the store.

"Oh, nothing."

Act nonchalant. We're just meeting a friend. Yaaayyyy, as her son would say!

Twenty minutes later Michael appeared at the meeting point for their adventure.

"Hi, Mike!" Andrew said, as if they were old friends.

"Hey, guys," he answered.

The boys were eating their candy.

"Where's mine?" Mike asked them.

"Your what?" Brandon replied.

"*Dude*, you were supposed to get me some M&Ms!" He put his hands on his hips and everyone laughed.

THEY HAD A fabulous time together that evening. Rachel was elated with this new relationship and how well the boys had taken to Michael. It had to be a dream. But it wasn't. She'd have to ask Erin to pinch her later on to make sure.

Everyone got back to the lodge in one piece, and Erin

pushed the button of the elevator that would take them upstairs to their rooms.

"One glass of wine?" Michael mouthed to Rachel pointing to the lounge as she got ready to board the elevator.

"How about a dance instead?" she whispered back.

I can't believe I just said that.

Erin got the message and ushered the boys onto the elevator.

When the elevator closed, Michael clutched Rachel's hand and accompanied her over to the night club entrance. The club was packed again, the same as the previous night, but they managed to squeeze by the people and onto the dance floor for their dance.

Fast music was playing. Darn. She had wanted it to be a slow dance. Michael must have read her mind.

"Come on. We'll make our own slow dance," he said.

They left the club and went back out into the lobby where they found a secluded corner by the large glass windows looking out onto the slopes. Some of the runs were lit for night skiing, and they watched the people going up in the lift and skiing down a few minutes later. Then Michael started humming a song. He extended his arms as if to motion asking for a dance. She complied, of course, greatly exaggerating her acceptance.

They danced as if they were in a ballroom swaying across a marbled floor, and after a few laughs, he pulled her close and she nestled her head in his neck as both swayed slowly to the soft music playing in the lobby. When the song was over, they held each other tightly and stared off into the distance at the slopes through the glass panes in front of them. He kissed her forehead; then her nose. He brushed his lips across her cheeks and then onto her mouth. It was tender and soft.

"Where are we going with this, Rachel?" he asked her quietly as he held her head against his chest.

Rachel had not expected that question. Ever. It had always been the woman who had needed reassurance about the future of a relationship, not the man. What was she supposed to say? She didn't have the answer! She had figured it would be okay to see where this desire would lead them, but she certainly wasn't ready to answer that question right now.

"I don't know," she whispered.

"I don't want to lose you again."

"Again?"

"Rachel, I loved you in high school as much as a teenager could love another teenager. I know it was a long time ago, and maybe it wasn't real. Eventually we all grow up and that type of young infatuation dissipates. But this, this we have right now, it isn't infatuation, Rachel. I never dreamed in a million years I'd ever see you again. I hadn't thought about you for many, many years. But when I saw you at the ski shop two days ago, every emotion came flooding back, and it knocked me off my feet. This time the feelings are those of a mature adult. This isn't a crush for me. It is real. And I don't want to go through the hurt, because this time would be different. I feel so strongly about you that I am willing to take a chance on anything; even on a *maybe*. Even if you give me the slightest chance of being with you. If you aren't ready, you need to let me know, and I will wait for as long as it takes. But if you don't ever want to hear from me after this trip, please tell me now."

She sighed. "Can we sit down and talk?"

They walked over to a stuffed beige couch in the lobby, away from any people, and they sat down. He held her hand preparing for the worst.

"Michael."

"It's okay," he said quickly. "I know I put you on the spot. You don't have to respond now. Just promise me if you realize you have any feelings for me, you will let me know someday, and you won't be afraid to find me."

"I *do* feel the same. But I can't say I'm not afraid, Michael. And I can't promise I'll go looking for you way out in California. I mean, I have kids, a job..." She looked down at his hand holding hers to avoid his eyes.

"Okay, then *I* will."

"You will what?"

"I will find you when you are ready."

She hugged him with every ounce of courage she had. She felt as if the door to her heart had been opened, even if it had been just a crack for now. *A big crack*, she thought.

"What is your favorite flower?" he unexpectedly asked.

"Gosh, my favorite flower? I guess I'd have to say sunflowers," she responded perplexed by the question.

"Why are they your favorite?"

"They're yellow, and they're happy flowers."

"I promise to bring you sunflowers. I promise to listen to you when you are sad, or angry, and to help you through tough times. I promise to make you happy, Rachel. And I will go as slow as you need with this."

"Okay," she said.

Okay.

She had her answer. He would be there. She had fallen in love, and it was clear to her now. But she wouldn't tell him yet. She knew he felt the same for her.

Two days. It had only been two days, and she had fallen in love that quickly!

Chapter 9

"SO, WHAT'S THE plan for today?" Erin asked Rachel at breakfast while the boys were at the buffet getting their food.

"Isn't Michael supposed to leave today? It *is* Sunday, right?"

"Yes, it's Sunday. I know, you kind of lose track of time here, don't you? But yes, he was here all of last week and said he was supposed to leave today. Then last night he told me he was going to extend his trip through Tuesday since we would still be here."

"Can he do that? I mean, just decide to stay on some extra days?"

"I guess he can do anything he wants since he's the owner of his law firm. But he said he's going to go home to spend Christmas with his daughter, so he'll have to leave on Tuesday for sure."

"Does he have a place to stay if he remains here for a couple more days?"

"Apparently the owner of the cottage said he could stay on because they're in the Caribbean somewhere, but he said he preferred to get a room here at the lodge for tonight and tomorrow night. He definitely has connections here!"

"That's good," Erin said eating a bit of her food.

"Anyway, Mike asked if we want to go cross-country skiing today. He thought it would be something different we could all do together. What do you think?"

"Sure! I'd love to try that! Easier than downhill skiing, right?"

"Well, a little easier," she said, drawing out her words. "But you still get pretty tired."

"I don't care. I'm in!"

THE WHOLE GROUP went cross-country skiing and they came back even more tired than the previous day, if at all possible. The boys went off to play some video games in the game room and then to the pool. Rachel and Erin went out into the village for some more shopping.

"He's in love with me, Erin."

"And you?"

"Maybe," she said cringing and looking away.

"Rachel, that's okay! Really. What are you worried about? The boys? The fact he lives way out in California?'

"Am I being unfaithful to Patrick's memory?"

"*Really*? That's all you've got?"

"Am I?"

"Absolutely not. If you had been the one to die, and Patrick had been the one to live on and have the kids, what would you have wanted him to do?"

They walked in silence for a moment. Rachel could hear the crunch of the snow under her feet.

"Okay. Okay."

"Okay, *what*? Say it."

"I would have wanted him to meet someone and to be happy. I would have wanted the boys to have a step-mom. If she was nice to them. Not if she was an evil step-mom."

"This isn't a fantasy world, it's reality. It's not like we're living in Cinderella-land with evil step-moms. And your life isn't over, Rachel. Patrick's is. I'm not trying to be crude. I mean, he was my brother-in-law and the father of those adorable twins. But when those boys grow up and get married, neither one of them is going to want their mom to come and live with them."

"Touché." Rachel laughed. "Okay, I get it. Live for today."

Erin cocked her head and looked at her suspiciously.

"No, I get it! Promise. I'm good."

"But..." Erin prodded.

"But he lives in CALIFORNIA, Erin! What am I supposed to do about that?"

"Here's the plan." She walked for a moment in silence looking down at the ground.

"Yes?" Rachel smiled.

"Okay, I'm working on it. Give me a minute."

Rachel and Erin both laughed and disappeared into a boutique like any typical woman would have if they had seen the same colorful and sparkly items in the display window as they had just spotted.

LATER IN THE evening, Michael had invited them all out to dinner at a little restaurant on the outskirts of the Olympic village called Caffe Rustica. It was a family-owned restaurant where they served European food that was to die for. He had tried to convince the boys to come with them because the Caffe had the best wood-fired oven pizza in town. But the boys were too tired, so they told their mom to go without them.

"Really?"

"Yeah, mom. Just go. It'll be fun. If the pizza is good, you can bring one back for us."

And that was that.

Rachel had bought one of those colorful tunics she had seen in the boutique in town, so she showered and changed into some black tights and the bright top. Michael had extended the contract on his rental car for a few more days and swung by the entrance of the lodge to pick her up.

At dinner they covered as much ground as possible probing into each other's lives as if they hadn't seen each other in decades. Well, they *hadn't* seen each other in decades. They talked about Michael's rise in the law business, his life in California, his recent ventures into movie production, and his desire to buy his own winery. Rachel was fascinated by his stories about the movies he had started producing. She was even more intrigued by his exploits to Africa and Argentina to visit wineries of those regions and learn about viticulture and grapes and the secrets that turned a good wine into a great wine.

Rachel felt as if she had not been able to contribute much to the conversation, because she had led such a mundane life compared to his. She got her degree, got married, became a teacher, had children, and that was it. Nothing too exciting, she had concluded. But Michael asked her questions about her teaching, about her students, about the foreign exchange program she had organized for her school, and about her own wishes to work in a winery. He asked about the boys' baseball games, the family camping trips, the time she and the boys went to Puerto Rico for Easter, and about their white-water rafting trips at Harper's Ferry in Virginia. By the time he had finished asking questions, she felt as if she had led an interesting and exciting life as well. One didn't have to go to Africa or produce a movie to feel accomplished in life.

"Mike, you don't have to answer this if you think it's too personal," she said.

"Nothing is too personal," he responded with a smile.

"You mentioned a couple days ago that your daughter Ellie had been conceived without your knowledge, and her mom had disappeared from college while you were in the hospital recuperating from your car accident."

"What would you like to know? It's important you know anything and everything you want to know, Rachel. I'm all yours."

"What ever happened to her mom? Did you find her and marry her? Or anyone else after that?"

"Hmm. Those were three questions in a row, so I'll start with the first one."

"Oh, I'm sorry! Am I being too nosey?"

"Never. Okay, Ellie's mom was named Grace. She came from a wealthy Catholic family that kept her sequestered from the real world all the way through high school."

"They kept her behind closed doors?"

"No, I didn't mean that. They just kept a tight rein on her, and they monitored her friends and calls and so forth."

"Got it."

"When Grace went to Stanford, she discovered a different life; a life of independence and choices. She became a bit of a hippy, as I mentioned before, and we spent a lot of time camping, hiking trails in the woods, making love, and smoking marijuana."

Rachel looked down at her plate after his last statement.

"Sorry, I guess that's too much information."

"No, it's okay. Go on."

"Grace was an artist, and a great one. I guess that's where Ellie gets her artistic streak. She's a fabulous illustrator. Anyway, Grace's family had wanted her to become a doctor or something more conformist, but she loved painting and drawing. She'd carry a tablet and pencil in a big old hippy shoulder bag, and everywhere she went, she'd break them out and just start drawing. She could be seated in a dentist's office, and she'd start drawing the children sitting across from her. We'd go camping in the woods for a weekend, and she would come back with the most beautiful creations."

He paused as if seeing the drawings before his eyes.

"Anyway," he continued, "Grace rejected the elitist life her parents had hoped she would embrace. When she got pregnant with Ellie, she figured she couldn't stay in college. I still don't understand why she didn't tell me about the baby; we could have worked it all out somehow. Maybe she thought I wasn't responsible enough at that point to be a father."

"Where did she go to have the baby?"

"The note she left me said she had gone home to her parents. But she hadn't. I think she tried, but they didn't want to have anything to do with her condition. Grace's older sister, Mary Katherine, told me her parents had tried to send her to some convent to hide until the baby was born, but Grace had refused to go. So Mary Katherine took her in."

"And she had the baby there?"

"Yes. I still hadn't been able to find her; I didn't even know Grace had a sister."

"So then what happened?"

"Are you sure you want to hear all of this?"

"Yes. I want to know all about you. Unless it's too personal, or it hurts you too much to talk about it."

"I want you to know anything you feel is important, Rachel. No secrets. I told you, I'm all yours and I mean it."

"No secrets," she repeated.

"Grace had the baby and lived with Mary Katherine in an apartment in Connecticut. She cleaned up her act and started taking art classes and doing odd jobs to help with the rent."

"Where is she now?"

"When Ellie was about two years old, Grace found out she had cancer. I still had no idea where she was. I had just continued living my life thinking she had broken up with me and had moved on with her own life. I thought maybe she had seen me as a dead-end boyfriend, because at the time we broke up, I was a pot-head with no goals or aspirations. The accident changed everything for me, but I never got the chance to tell her in person. She knew, though. She apparently kept informed about me, somehow, maybe through friends, and she knew I was headed to law school. That's when she died."

"Oh, my goodness!" Rachel exclaimed putting both hands up to her mouth and then looking around the restaurant to see if anyone had heard her.

"Mary Katherine called me right after her sister died. Grace had made her promise to not contact me until then. I was twenty-three. Ellie was three years old, and I had just graduated from college and was in my first year of law school."

"What did you do then?"

"I cried a lot. I was heartbroken Grace had had to go through all of that on her own. But I was elated at knowing I had a little girl. I wasn't mad at Grace for not telling me, but I was definitely hurt. She left me a long letter explaining her reasons for leaving me and keeping Ellie a secret, but I'll keep that private, if that's okay."

"Of course! Of course, Mike. I am so sorry..."

"She left Ellie some wonderful journals to read as she got older, and some beautiful drawings and paintings of her as a baby. It helped me see Ellie's development through Grace's artwork, since I had lost those three years. She had even drawn a picture of herself pregnant by looking into a mirror reflecting her large belly." He smiled. "Ellie loves that one."

"Has she read her mom's journals yet?"

"Yes. We don't keep any secrets from each other. I started reading her mom's letters to her when she was little. Ellie is so much like her mom. She has her long curly hair and big brown eyes, and she is such a free spirit. She's mature beyond her age, and smart. I'm very fortunate, and very proud of her."

"Did Ellie live with you while you attended law

school?"

"Yep. Just dad and his little pixie! Well, we got a dog, too."

"Was that difficult?"

"Most difficult thing I've ever done and the most rewarding." He looked at her and smiled. "So is there anything else you want to know?"

"Did you ever fall in love or get married to anyone after that?"

"No marriage. I'm not sure Grace and I would have gotten married either, to tell you the truth. We cared about each other very much, but our relationship was just one of those young free-spirited things you get into. She knew it too, and that was part of the reason for her not telling me about the pregnancy. Anyway, after my relationship with Grace, I was focused on graduating from college and then getting through law school. There were a few long-termed relationships, but I hadn't met anyone I couldn't live without."

"Hadn't?"

"What?" he asked perplexed.

"You said you *hadn't* met anyone," Rachel repeated.

"Until now," he said as he took her hand in his and kissed it.

They sat there in silence for a moment as Rachel tried to digest all the information Michael had shared with her that evening.

Michael had been hurt deeply in his past, and he had lost someone just as she had, even though he may not have loved Grace as much as she had loved Patrick. *But he gets it*, she thought to herself. *He gets it.*

"Come on; let's go back to the lodge. It's getting late," he said.

BACK AT THE lodge, there had been no discussion about it; they had both spontaneously gone up in the elevator to his room.

"Wow," she exclaimed as she walked through the door to his suite, "I have never seen a room this elegant in my life!"

"I know. They spoil me here. It's the equivalent of a penthouse, except there's no penthouse here. Just the luxury suite," he explained with a smile. "I really don't try to live like this, by the way. I stay in regular hotel rooms, I drive regular cars, and I own a modest house."

"They must think you are pretty special."

"Well, it's more like there were no other rooms available at the last minute, so I told them I'd take whatever they had."

"You did this for me? You took this room so you could stay a few extra days?"

"Yes, ma'am!" he answered while grabbing her in a big bear hug and lifting her off the floor for a twirl. "Come over here to the glass doors. The view is really spectacular!"

He pushed the curtains aside and Rachel gasped at the magnificence of Mirror Lake below. The ice reflected the bright colors of the Christmas lights nearby: yellows, reds, greens, and blues. She could see tiny figures skating in a roped-off section of the lake. There were faint wispy designs being carved into the ice by the skaters as they glazed across its surface.

"Glass of champagne?" he asked holding up a bottle of *Veuve Clicquot.*

"Gosh, you really *do* rate around here!"

"It comes with the room. Can't let it go to waste, right?" he asked tilting his head.

He went over to uncork the bottle and look for two champagne flutes, while Rachel remained by the glass doors and stared at the lights and figures below.

"The sunrise is even prettier than this," he said. "You'll have to see it."

"Okay."

Okay. She was going to stay.

After a few glasses of champagne, Michael turned off the table lamps. He enveloped Rachel in his arms as the delicate light of the moon tiptoed into the room. He gently tugged at her tunic as he kissed her face and her neck. She didn't object. He pulled the tunic over her head as she lifted her arms, and then she pulled off her tights.

Thank God I wore nice underwear, she thought.

He began unbuttoning his shirt until Rachel swatted at his hand and took over. She couldn't believe her courage. She tentatively unbuttoned with one hand and took a sip of her champagne with the other.

"One-handed?" he teased with a smile.

She blushed and then put the champagne flute down to finish unbuttoning his shirt. She slipped his shirt off his shoulders and it fell to the floor. He pointed to his belt buckle and a questioning look formed on his brow. She unbuckled his belt and then his slacks, but she couldn't bring herself to unzip his pants. He did the honors himself, and as his pants fell to the ground, she quickly covered her eyes with her hand.

Michael laughed and stepped out of his trousers. He picked up his shirt from the floor and handed it to Rachel.

"Here, it's cold. Sorry I don't have any pajamas to offer you."

Rachel was shivering, but it had nothing to do with the temperature in the room. She put on his shirt and was seduced once again by the smell of his cologne on its collar.

They stood there for a moment; Rachel in his buttoned-down shirt, and he in his boxers and white t-shirt. She snuck a glance at his boxers and laughed out loud.

"What? You don't think bears on boxers are attractive? Were you expecting fish, or ducks?"

They both laughed.

"Guess I'm just a practical guy. I don't do silk," he said with a smile.

"The bears are fine!"

"Here, call Erin so she won't worry," he said with a smile as he handed her his cell phone from the counter nearby. "I'm going to pour us the rest of the champagne."

Rachel thought she saw a skip in his step as he went over to the counter, and she knew he was as excited as she. This was a break-through for her. She hadn't opened her heart to anyone for years, and now she knew how. It was clear.

A few minutes later, they lay down on the over-sized couch facing the view of the lake beyond the windows. He had thrown off the decorative cushions to make more room, and with his back against the couch, he held Rachel close to him under a blanket.

His body was so warm, she reflected. He was quite athletic; something she had not seen through all the winter layers he had been wearing. She felt his sturdy arms holding her close to him as the last remnants of hesitation and doubt drained from her body.

His legs intertwined with hers.

Had she shaved her legs?

She could hear the rhythm of his heartbeat as she laid her head on his chest. She kissed his neck and he lightly caressed her hair and rubbed her back. Eventually they fell asleep there.

RACHEL WAS STARTLED into consciousness as Michael tried to gradually pry himself out of her arms the next morning.

"Shh," he said. "It's okay. I just want you to see the sunrise over the lake."

She stretched her arms and rubbed her eyes and tried to get her bearings as she sat up on the couch.

"You okay, sleepy-head?" he asked her smiling.

"Yeah. What time is it?"

"Early. I wanted to make sure you got up in time to sneak back to your room before your boys get up and go looking for you."

"Okay…"

"Come here and take a look at these colors in the sky."

"Oh, it's beautiful, Michael!"

"Just like you."

He slowly turned her around and kissed her delicately on the lips. As he drew away, she pulled his face back to hers and gently bit his bottom lip as she kissed him and ran her hands through his hair. He drew her so close to him that every inch of their barely clad bodies touched and burned with desire. He kissed her hard, parting her lips and exploring her mouth. She instinctively jumped up and wrapped her legs around his waist, and he carried her over to the bedroom and laid her on the bed. They grabbed at each other's clothing until there was nothing left between them. He rolled over on top of her and looked into her eyes for a long moment. He didn't want to take advantage; only to love.

"Are you sure, Rachel?"

"Yes."

Chapter 10

"ERIN, WAKE UP!" Rachel demanded of her sister-in-law as she jumped on her bed.

"*What? What?*" she asked as she came out of a deep sleep. "What's wrong?!"

"I slept with him!" she squealed and clasped both her hands in front of her face like a little child.

"Oh my God, Rachel, tell me!!!"

"Shh! The boys are next door."

Rachel grabbed Erin and hugged her and then pushed her away so she could tell her more.

"I told him I love him, too."

"Rach, I am so happy for you! But wait, I have to go pee," Erin said jumping off the bed and running into the bathroom. "Then you have to tell me all about it!" her voice echoed in the tiled room.

IT WAS MONDAY morning; one more day with Michael before he would be returning to California. Rachel had invited him to go with her and the boys that morning on a dog-sled trip, but he had politely declined explaining he had some work to do on his laptop and some conference calls to make. His firm was starting a new case he expected would be complex and tedious, and he had needed to get the ball rolling with his associates until he could get back to the office to take over.

They had agreed to meet at three o'clock to discuss how they would keep their long-distance relationship going until they could figure out what the future would look like. She figured she'd also ask Michael if he could fly to Virginia for Darlene's wedding in the summer. By then the boys would surely know about their romance.

After the dog-sled ride, everyone returned to the lodge and changed clothes for their afternoon of skiing. They would be turning in their rentals on Wednesday morning before leaving for Syracuse, so they had wanted to take advantage of their last two days on the slopes.

"Erin, which slope are you going to begin on today?" Rachel asked, as they headed towards the lobby's exit.

"I think I'll go down Boreen run once or twice before getting back to the intermediate slopes. Why?"

"Can you take the boys there to get warmed up with you, and then I'll join everyone in about thirty minutes on the intermediate slopes?"

"Ha! I know what you're going to do!" she sang to her sister-in-law and gave her a sly look.

"I'm only going to go say hi, and that's it! He's working, okay? I promise I'll be out there in half an hour to meet you."

"Yeah, right!"

"Really! Keep your cell phone on. And don't let the boys convince you to go to any other slopes until I get there."

"Okay. Good hunting!"

"Oh my gosh, you are such a..., such a..." she couldn't find the right words.

"Such a *great* sister-in-law?" They both laughed as Erin ushered the trio of boys out the door and over to the chair lift to go up the mountain.

Rachel waved from the door and turned to go back inside. She walked towards the bank of elevators she knew would take her to Michael's floor. Before she could reach them, however, she noticed a group of animated people rushing towards the reception desk nearby. She wondered what the commotion was about.

No sooner had she decided to walk over and see what was going on, she saw Tyra Milano, the movie star from *Dancing in the Wind,* checking in at the reception desk. Everyone appeared to be bending over backwards to help her, and a small crowd of autograph-seekers had congregated to shake hands and see if they could get a picture of themselves with the icon. Rachel had recognized her immediately from her photos in the tabloids. Tyra Milano was as stunning as she had been portrayed.

Ms. Milano had a young teenage girl with her, whom Rachel assumed to be her daughter, as she shared the same warm light brown skin the African-American star had. Both of them wore their hair up in loose buns with curls cascading down the sides of their faces. They were dressed in tight jeans with tank tops and fur-collared coats.

The scene made Rachel wish her own daughter had

survived, even though she knew in her heart God had not intended for her to have a third child to raise after Patrick had died. Nevertheless, seeing Ms. Milano and her daughter link arms and interact spiritedly with the fans brought back a longing she had set aside several years ago. Elizabeth, as she had prematurely named the baby, was with her father in Heaven; she just knew it to be true.

Tyra had always been portrayed by the press as a gracious movie star who had been appreciative and respectful of her fans. Talk show hosts had vied for her time, as she was entertaining and glamorous and very down-to-earth. She never came across as narcissistic. Probably every man in town had fantasized about dating Tyra Milano at one point or another, and now Rachel could see why.

Rachel had been standing in a corner near the reception desk tucked away from the spectacle, and she had not heard the elevators open nor seen Michael walk past her toward the gathering. That is, until he reached Ms. Milano and her entourage.

Michael was beaming as he walked up to the teenage girl and hugged her and kissed her on the forehead. It appeared there was a certain familiarity between them. Did he know Ms. Milano and her daughter that well? The star unexpectedly leaned over and kissed Michael full on the mouth. He reciprocated with a big hug and another kiss. He held her in his arms and his eyes were bright with excitement as he spoke to her. Rachel couldn't hear the words, of course, but she certainly could see there was a strong emotional bond shared by the twosome.

This doesn't look like a greeting between friends, she thought. *Is this Michael's lover, or his fiancé?*

Rachel suddenly felt her heart racing as she continued to observe the scene unfolding in front of her. Her mind tried hopelessly to sort out the confusion. Michael continued holding on to the star's waist as he responded to questions from the reporters who had appropriated the lobby. Rachel watched as he grabbed the younger girl again and ruffled the curls on her head. The paparazzi were flashing cameras from all angles, and Tyra overtly flirted with Michael and the photographers for their collection of shots. He responded to her advances by pulling her closer.

Had this whole week with Michael been a farce? Was the movie star really his girlfriend? Could Michael have lured her in with his sad story about returning to the lodge each year to fulfill a family promise, all the while exploiting her vulnerability so he could get her into bed while his fiancé was off somewhere promoting her new movie?

She started to think back on their days together, picking apart their conversations, searching for indications he may have been deceiving her. *No, not Michael,* she thought. *I'm overreacting.* Michael was an honest man; she just knew it.

She realized she had never asked if he was currently involved with anyone; she had just assumed he wasn't. He had never offered the information, and she had never thought to probe. But surely a man of his stature in society, one with his wealth and looks, could be involved with someone the likes of Tyra Milano, right? What if Ms. Milano was in fact his girlfriend, and he had fallen in love with Rachel, and he had intended on breaking up with the star when he returned to California? And then she had surprised him with this unexpected visit…

It was a plausible scenario, wasn't it?

Does that make me the other woman? The one who wrecked this idyllic union between the super-star and her powerful lawyer? I don't want to be the other woman! I don't want my picture in the press!

Michael continued holding onto the woman while conversing ardently with her and her entourage. Circumstances and consequences cascaded through Rachel's mind as she tried unsuccessfully to create a situation that would make sense of it all.

And then she heard it.

"Hey you two lovebirds," the photographer said, "come over here by the fireplace to get a better picture for the magazine cover."

She gasped as both her hands rushed to her mouth to keep her from crying out loud. She turned to rush out of the main lobby door hoping not to be seen, but it was too late. Michael had seen her.

"Rachel!" he called out to her from where he stood by the fireplace.

Rachel looked at him for a second, then at a perplexed Tyra, and she bolted out the door.

"No, Rachel, come here!" she heard him exclaim behind her.

When she got outside, she was dazed and couldn't remember what she had told Erin. Was she supposed to call her or just meet her at the top of the mountain? Was it a bad idea in her state of mind to go skiing right now? Maybe she should just go up the lift and try to disappear into the crowd until she could sort out her feelings and stop crying enough to greet her children and sister-in-law. The pain was intense. She doubled over with both arms wrapped around her chest.

She was falling apart...

Rachel didn't hear Michael rush up behind her, but she felt his hand on her shoulder as he turned her around.

"Rachel, were you in the lobby?"

"I saw, Mike. I saw you kissing Tyra Milano back there."

She couldn't help crying, even though she hadn't wanted to give Michael the pleasure of seeing how he had hurt her.

"Rachel, I can explain."

"Then explain."

"This isn't the place or the time."

"Did you sleep with her too, Mike?"

"Rachel..."

"Answer me! Did you sleep with her too?"

"Yes, but it's complicated."

"I can't wait to hear the explanation."

"I can't explain it right now, Rachel. You just have to trust me."

"Good-bye, Michael."

"No, Rachel, you need to hear me out."

"I don't need to hear anything, Michael. You lied to me."

At that very moment, Rachel heard her cell phone ring in her pocket. She put the phone to her ear and turned to leave as she took the call.

"Rachel," Erin said on the other line, "it's me. Andrew had a fall, and it doesn't look good. He may have broken his leg or his ankle; it's hard to tell."

"Oh my God!" Rachel responded. "Where is he?!"

"The medics took him down the mountain on the sled and he should be getting to the bottom any moment now. They are taking him to the hospital. They told me to call you and tell you to meet them at that big building beside the lodge where we saw the red cross on the door yesterday. You can ride to the hospital with them in the ambulance."

"Okay, I'm headed there now. You stay with Brad and Brandon at the lodge while I go to the hospital," she said breathing deeply between her sobs. "And keep your phone on. Erin, thanks. Really."

"I'm so sorry," her sister-in-law said on the phone.

"No, it's not your fault, Erin. I've got to go. I'll keep in touch."

"What is it, Rachel? Who is going to the hospital? Who was hurt?" Michael asked with a genuinely frenetic look in his eyes.

"It's none of your worry, Michael. You go back to your friends."

"Rachel," he said holding onto her arm.

"Leave it alone," she brushed his hand off. "Just go, Michael. Just go."

She turned and left. He knew he had to let her go.

Chapter 11

ANDREW HAD INDEED broken his ankle, but nothing the medics hadn't seen before. It was a minor break that could easily be set without invasive surgery, and he'd have to wear a cast for six to eight weeks.

That was not the issue. The doctors told Rachel something else seemed to be going on in Andrew's body; something that could be seriously wrong. He would need tests. She could stay at the hospital there, go to the hospital in Syracuse, or go to her hospital back home in Virginia for the tests. She decided to go to Syracuse to have the ankle set, and then return home for the tests.

Erin had packed up their things at the lodge and had turned in the ski rental equipment. She had driven the car and the two boys to meet Rachel at the hospital three hours later. The doctors had just finished wrapping Andrew's ankle and had given him medication to reduce the pain and swelling. The nurse had given him some ice-packs for their trip back to Syracuse in the car. He'd have to check into the hospital in Syracuse in a couple of days to have the ankle set after the swelling went down and to get his cast put on. Then they would head back to Virginia to make appointments for the tests the doctors had recommended. Rachel had no idea what the doctor's had been concerned about. Andrew's undiagnosed condition had no name yet, only symptoms.

Chapter 12

RACHEL SAT IN the waiting room at the Virginia Commonwealth University Massey Cancer Center which was a little over an hour away from her home in Virginia. Andrew had been diagnosed with aplastic anemia, a bone marrow deficiency, where the immune system mistakenly destroys bone marrow. The doctors had explained that it could have been something he had inherited, or it could have been brought on by a viral infection. They had asked Rachel to try to find Patrick's medical records and those of his biological parents, to make the determination of the cause.

In any case, the doctors had determined Andrew would need an allogeneic bone marrow transplant, in which the donor's stem cells would be introduced to replace Andrew's stem cells, thus rebuilding a healthier immune system. Once the diseased bone marrow was replaced with healthy bone marrow from a donor, the disease would probably be cured, especially since he was so young and they had detected it so early on.

All family members had been tested for a match by having a DNA swab taken from the inside of their cheek.

Brandon was the only candidate with matching DNA eligible to be the donor. Having a sibling as the donor would produce even better outcomes.

The doctors had assured Brandon the procedure would be quite simple, and it would cause little more than slight bruising and discomfort for him. It would be an in-and-out of hospital procedure. He'd donate on a Friday and be back at school on a Monday. Not that Brandon wanted to go back to school so quickly.

The doctors had continued to explain there would be no risk to Brandon's health, and his body would recreate the lost marrow stem cells quickly. Brandon never hesitated to offer himself as a donor for his brother. Rachel had cried not only for Andrew, but for Brandon and his selfless gift to his brother.

The Bone Marrow Transplant program at VCU was one of the best in Virginia, and Rachel considered herself fortunate to live so close by the center. They would offer a follow-up team that would continue to check-in with Andrew every now and then for the next ten years and beyond, if necessary, just to make sure his good health continued.

Only a parent understands the pain and agony of having something like this happen to a child, Rachel believed. She had sat in the waiting room of the hospital when they had been diagnosing Andrew's case, begging God to take her instead of her son. And yet, she knew she had to stay on earth to take care of Brandon. When she found out the prognosis and cure, she thanked God multiple times every day for not taking her child. The doctor's had assured her Andrew would be fine after the transplant. His recovery period would be short, and his future would be guaranteed.

Rachel wondered how Andrew had come across this disease. Had he contracted a virus from someone? Would Brandon be susceptible as well? Surely if it had been a virus, it would have already shown up in Brandon. So it had to have been inherited, she concluded. But Rachel's family had no known history of any immune system disorder. It must have come from Patrick's family.

Patrick had been adopted at an early age, so he hadn't delved too deeply into the medical histories of his biological parents. He had requested medical records from each of them when he had joined the Air Force, but he hadn't shared anything significant about the reports with Rachel. She remembered Patrick had kept the documents in a folder somewhere in his office desk, so she decided to look for them in order to have a comprehensive medical account to share with her son's doctors.

ONE EVENING WHEN she returned from the hospital, Rachel opened the door to Patrick's study and wandered over to the antique chair at his desk. He had loved that chair, as wobbly as it was. He had found it in some horse barn during his college days, and he had cherished it all the years since then. There was probably a story behind it, one Rachel didn't know, but she felt Patrick would have wanted her to keep the aged treasure.

It had been a long time since she had been in his office. She sat there for a few moments with her arms extended across his shiny mahogany desk, and then she put her head down and quietly sobbed.

Rachel carefully opened the drawers of her husband's

desk where she still had most of his old papers and a few
files the Air Force had returned to her following Patrick's
death. She stared down at the files and felt as if she were
spying on his life. She would have to go through the files
sooner or later; she had just not found the time to do it yet.
Or maybe she hadn't made the time. Slowly she leafed
through the tabs and came to one with the title *Medical
History*. Patrick had always been so organized. She looked
through the file and found the records she had needed for
the hospital. Nothing seemed unusual. There was no mention of bone marrow issues for either of his biological parents. And yet, Patrick's father had died young, so perhaps
he had been carrying the gene and hadn't known it.

Rachel glanced once more into the drawer as she was
closing it, and she saw the manila envelope the Air Force
had given her containing Patrick's passport and various
personal items he had carried with him on his trip to Bahrain. She opened the drawer wider and took out the envelope. She held the envelope in her hands for several
minutes, and then she gently unfastened the clasp and
poured the contents out onto the mahogany desk.

She opened Patrick's passport to the page containing
his picture, and she looked at it for a long time. She wondered if his image would blur in her mind as the years
passed. She also wondered if she was doing a good enough
job of trying to keep his image alive in the minds of their
children.

*When do you stop thinking about the loss of a loved
one?*

Rachel had believed Michael was her answer. She had
fallen in love with him in those four short days together.

And it hadn't been infatuation. It had been deep and intimate.

Is it possible to fall in love with two people in a lifetime?

It suddenly felt chilly in the room, and she rubbed her arms to bring some warmth to her body as she sat there in deep thought.

She hadn't had any time to think about Michael and the events at Lake Placid for the past month; life had been so crazy. But as she sat there recreating the tender loving moments they had shared at the resort, her thoughts were continually interrupted and replaced by the image of Michael kissing Tyra Milano. She remembered her last question for him: *did you sleep with her?* She couldn't believe he had made love to her that very morning while engaged in a relationship with the star. Had he been thinking of Ms. Milano as he made love to her? Had he been comparing the dazzling vivacious star to *her*, a mom of two and a teacher? How could she compete with that goddess? She couldn't. She wouldn't. What was the point of even thinking about it? He was in California. She was in Virginia. She had children to take care of and a job to do, even though she had taken a leave of absence from teaching until Andrew improved.

Rachel looked at the other items lying on the desk from the envelope: Patrick's birth certificate, a receipt from the cleaners, his keys, some gum, and the medals from his uniform. All the other items had been returned in the suitcase Patrick had taken with him to Bahrain. Rachel picked up the medals and ran her fingers over the inscriptions on the back. They all stood for honor, valor, and bravery. She would make sure to give her son's these medals as keep-sakes when they were older. She threw the packet of gum in the trash. She figured the receipt for the cleaners was long overdue, so she threw that away as well. She picked up his set of keys and went through each one. Patrick would have held these keys. She came to a small key she didn't recognize, and she wondered what it belonged to. It wasn't a mailbox key. Maybe a key to the bicycle lock? Or an extra key to their shed in the back? She'd have to check. She took the key off the ring and put it in her pocket. Then she replaced the items in the envelope and filed them back in the drawer of his desk. She walked out of the room slow-ly carrying the medical file, and she turned off the light. She looked in one more time, as if wishing Patrick to ap-pear.

Why did you die, Patrick? Why did you leave us?

Chapter 13

"HI, RACHEL!" DARLENE exclaimed on the other side of the phone. "Happy birthday, girl!"

"Thanks, Darlene," Rachel replied with a smile. "I had forgotten it was my birthday."

"Don't give me that crap. We're going out today."

"What are you talking about? I have the boys!"

"Yeah, but on Tuesday you told me they were going to their grandmother's house this afternoon and you were celebrating your birthday with them tomorrow," she replied. "Aha! You see how I remembered? So we're going out."

"Okay, you caught me. But I don't want to be reminded about how old I'm getting! So don't take me to any Mexican restaurant where they make you wear some big sombrero while they sing *Feliz Cumpleaños*."

"You are *such* a party-pooper! Get ready. I'll pick you up at one."

"Okay. And I want to hear all the latest on the wedding plans. I feel like I haven't seen you in *years*."

Andrew had been home from the hospital for over a month, and everyone was back at school. Both boys were thriving and had returned to their old selves. It was Rachel who still worried; who still prepared every day for some type of catastrophic event. She couldn't shake the feeling of an impending loss lurking around the corner. She knew in her rational mind the boys were well; they both had been given a clean bill of health. She wasn't married, so there was no husband to lose again. She wasn't pregnant, so there was no baby to lose. And there was no Michael Blanford. Nothing to lose. And yet, the feeling was still there in the shadows. It haunted her. It made her do silly things like prepare a detailed list of all the magazines she was subscribed to and record in a notebook the addresses of all the bills she would pay each month. She made a list of her friends and their contact numbers in case someone should need it. She had folders with the detailed medical history for her and the boys. Everything was in order. Everything was ready; just in case…

She had thought she was going to lose another child three short months ago when Andrew had been diagnosed with his disease. She had nurtured that child through all his little colds when he was growing up; she had read him stories every night with his brother as they sat on the floor next to their beds; she had never missed any of his little Valentine's Day and Halloween parties at school, and she had always made him his favorite *Funfetti* cupcakes for his birthday. All of that could have been taken away from her if he had not fallen off those skis and had not been taken to the hospital for an unrelated injury to his ankle. There had to have been an angel watching over him. Maybe it was Patrick, in some ethereal way.

DARLENE PICKED RACHEL up at about one o'clock. They were going to look at the last few wineries on her list for the wedding venue, and they'd celebrate Rachel's birthday with a glass of wine while they were at it.

Oliver had wanted to go too. Not that he was a wino. In any case, they had thrown the dog in the back and had opened up some windows so he could stick his head out and have his ears flop around in the wind. Why dogs enjoyed that was a mystery. Women certainly didn't appreciate having their hair blown about by the wind.

"I think I found the place for my wedding, Rach. But I had one more winery on my list, the Kaboyashi Winery. Have you ever been there?"

"Yes; it was a long time ago, though. It's nice, but I think it's small."

"Should we skip it, then?"

"We can check it out if you want, but I really don't think they have the space for what you have in mind. Have you narrowed down your other choices?"

"I think so. Barrel Oak said they'd figure out something for us on their grounds with a big tent if we decide to do it there. It sounds like they have the capacity for more people than I had thought. But there's also a new winery opening up this summer that I'm seriously considering, and they said they'd give me a great deal since my wedding would be their first big event."

"Where is it?"

"Do you remember the Lotus Winery? The one being sold by the older retired couple?"

"Yeah."

"Well, it sold."

"When?"

"February," Darlene responded. "I went over there one day to check it out, and it's really pretty. It's huge, too. There's a large stone fireplace as you walk in, and nice ambient lighting; very romantic. They have these large wooden bars in four or five rooms where you can go and taste the different varieties."

"Varietals," Rachel corrected her.

"Snob," she retorted with a smile.

"Hey, I'm just practicing the jargon! I'm seriously thinking about trying to get a job at a winery this summer, Darlene."

"Really?"

"Really. I mean, I've been talking about it for the past two years, so it's time I just do it."

"I think that's a great idea!"

"Yeah, it makes sense. The boys are getting ready to go to high school in the fall, so they're old enough to be on their own for a couple of hours. Plus they'll be in camps for half of the summer anyway. And they're going on a two-week trip with their grandparents to Arizona. So I just figured I needed something to keep me busy while they are gone."

"Good thinking! Do you have any idea where you would like to work?"

"Not yet, but I'm going to ask the folks at Barrel Oak if they need any pourers for the summer, or if they know of anyone who does. Surely it gets busy at the wineries around here in the summer, don't you think? With all the tourists?"

"Probably." Darlene nodded.

"And…" Rachel paused deliberately with a scheming

smile sneaking onto her face.

"And what?"

"Well, I know you are pushing for me to pick up dating again so I can find someone to take to your wedding. So I thought..." she trailed off leaving her friend to finish the sentence.

"So you thought this would be a way to meet someone."

"Right? I mean, wineries would probably attract the type of men I would be interested in, and certainly some of them have got to be single."

"Now you're talking!" her friend said animatedly.

As they drove the last few miles towards the Barrel Oak Winery, Darlene suddenly slowed the car.

"Look!" she said pointing out the window. "Someone is painting over the sign for the Lotus Winery. The new owners must be changing the name. Let's stop and check it out."

"Are they open for business to the public already?"

"I doubt it. But I'm sure they'll let us look around and you can tell me if you think this one should be at the top of my list for the wedding sites. It's my favorite so far."

"Okay, it can't hurt to ask."

They pulled the car next to the person who was painting over the sign near the road.

"Is the winery open to the public yet?" Darlene asked her while rolling down her window.

"Not yet," the young lady answered as she stood up and brushed some unruly strands of hair out of her face. She was holding a can of bright yellow paint in one hand, and a brush in the other.

She was tall and slender with warm brown skin, and she had long curly hair with a few bright red highlights to mark her individuality. She looked to be in her early twenties, and she wore jeans and a lilac sweatshirt with Moore College imprinted on the front.

She walked over to the car when she saw Oliver wagging his tail at her from the back seat. "I think your dog wants to say hi. Okay to pet him?"

"Sure!" Rachel responded.

Oliver was such a flirt.

"I spoke to someone a few weeks ago about maybe renting your place for my wedding in late August," Darlene said. "Is there any chance of showing my friend the inside of the winery?"

"Sure. I remember you. You're the lady that wants magenta and purple for her wedding colors, right?"

"You picked your colors already, and you didn't tell me?" Rachel turned to her friend and feigned shock.

"Hey, you haven't been around, so don't give me a hard time! Purple and magenta. You like that?"

"I love it!"

"I can meet you at the winery if you want to look around," the young lady said. "Let me put the top on this can and pick up a few things out here, and then I'll meet you inside to answer your questions."

Rachel and Darlene parked the car and walked toward the winery. It was tucked into lush wooded surroundings adjacent to rolling vineyards still sleeping from the long winter months. They walked up the stone path escorted by bushes that were beginning to show their buds. Surely they would reveal their colors in another several weeks, and Rachel was betting some of the flowers would be bright yellow like the paint the young owner was using on the sign. That is, if this young lady was in fact one of the proprietors.

They turned the heavy metal door knob and entered through the wooden passage to the main lobby. There was a glint of light shining through colorful panes of stained glass behind an exquisite hand-carved Redwood bar. An air of nostalgia filled the room for an era Rachel couldn't quite identify. She felt as if she had stepped into an old Frank Sinatra song. The room was bursting with delicious smells of currants and tobacco, even though the winery had been closed since the previous fall.

"Come here, I want to show you something," Darlene said gesturing to her right.

Rachel followed her friend over to an ornate wooden window frame and gazed out onto a covered stone terrace.

"Wow. Look at that beautiful brick fireplace on the terrace!"

"Right? They have a nice lawn too. They said they could set up rows of white wooden folding chairs, and then they'd have an arch with flowers where we'd stand to take our vows. I'm going to have a friend of mine play the wedding march on a harp."

"Would the reception be out there or inside?"

"On the terrace. But if it rains, we might move it inside."

"It really is beautiful here, Darlene. What I have seen so far looks perfect."

"Maybe they'll let us walk around so you can see the rest of the place. It really is beyond description."

"What are the wines like?" Rachel whispered to her

friend hoping the Moore College lady wouldn't hear.

"I don't know," Darlene whispered back.

"Do you want to taste them?" the lady covered in yellow paint asked as she came up behind them with the can of paint still in her hand.

"Um, I think you have some yellow paint in your hair," Rachel couldn't resist saying.

"You're right, the yellow was uninvited; the red is mine!" They all laughed.

"Do you own this winery?" Rachel asked.

"My family does. I guess that means I do too. So did you have a chance to look around?"

"A little," Darlene answered.

"Are you the two getting married?"

"Oh, no!" Rachel said rather quickly. "She's getting married, and I'm just the friend."

"Okay! Well, let me show you around and then we can taste some wine."

"Are you sure it's okay?" Darlene asked.

"Of course!" the yellow and red-haired lady answered.

"By the way, I'm Darlene and this is Rachel."

They all shook hands.

"I'm Elizabeth," she responded.

ELIZABETH SHOWED THEM around the winery and talked to them about the plans for some remodeling and marketing, the types of wines they wanted to continue producing, and the types of grapes they wanted to import for experiments of their own.

"We're still getting to know all the spots where the

vines are planted, and the rootstock and clones that already exist," Elizabeth explained.

"Did you have to get a new winemaker?" Rachel asked.

"No, we asked the current one if he wanted to stay on, and he said yes. We were pretty lucky to get him, because we don't know enough yet about these vines and grapes. But we did hire another winemaker from California to manage the day-to-day operations."

They came out of another nook where there were antiquated iron tables and charming stuffed arm chairs on terracotta-tiled floors.

"You have a lot of tasting rooms in here," Rachel said, fascinated by the enormity and splendor of the winery.

"I know, isn't it cool? We have five independent tasting rooms in this winery, and each one has a different personality," Elizabeth responded with not a hint of arrogance about her parent's affluence. "Come on; let me see if we have any bottles open for tasting. If not, what would you like me to open?"

"Which wines would you typically serve at a wedding?" Darlene asked.

"I don't have too much experience with that," she answered, "but we can try a few favorites, and then you can come back and ask my dad and the winemaker what they would recommend."

Rachel and Darlene sat at the hand-carved bar and Elizabeth got them two glasses. She uncorked a Chambourcin. "I'm sorry it hasn't had time to breathe," she said.

"Hey," Darlene responded, "*I'm* breathing, so this is just fine!" They all laughed.

After a few tastes of some of the wines, Rachel inquired about possibly working there in the summer. Elizabeth said she would give the information to the winemaker who was doing the hiring if she wished to leave her phone number. Rachel scrounged around in her large purse for a pen and something to write on. She found a piece of paper and a pen and began writing her number down when she heard a thud. Her purse had fallen off the stool beside her and had barely missed Oliver, who had been sitting patiently on the floor wondering if they served treats at this winery as well.

Rachel slipped off her stool, picked up the items scattered on the floor, and tossed them carelessly back into her purse. As she did so, she noticed the key she had thrown in her purse some weeks ago; the one she had found on Patrick's key chain when she had been looking for his medical records in his desk drawer.

"Hey," she asked Darlene, "do you know what this key is for?"

"What do you mean?"

"It was on Patrick's keychain, and for the life of me, I have no idea what it could be."

"I do. It's a bank deposit box key."

"Are you sure?" she asked turning it around in her hand. "But we don't have a bank deposit box."

"It looks like you do now!"

BY THE END of their visit, Rachel was totally enamored with the spectacular structure of the winery, the earthy vineyard, Elizabeth's cordiality, and the establishment's

Cabernet Franc and Viognier.

"Did you like it, Rach?"

"Loved it! I think that's the place, Darlene. *I* would get married there."

"Watch what you ask for!" her friend responded shaking a finger at her.

Chapter 14

THE KEY TO the safe deposit box was nagging at Rachel. Had Patrick mentioned it before, and she had just forgotten it? She knew the boys' birth certificates and all their important papers were in the files in Patrick's desk in the den, so why would he need a safe deposit box? It's not like they ever talked about protecting their documents from a fire or flood. And she didn't have any jewels to put in a safe deposit box.

The Monday following her visit to the winery with Darlene, Rachel went to her bank.

"Hello. My name is Rachel Matthews and my husband and I have an account here. My husband passed away three years ago, but I think he had a safe deposit box here."

"Oh, I'm sorry to hear about your husband," the teller said.

"Thanks. Anyway, it was long ago, so I don't know if you would still have the things in his box; if he in fact had a box here."

"You're not sure if he did?"

"No."

"Do you know what number the box might be?"

"I have this key, and it has the number eleven forty-two on it. Does that help?"

"Yes," the teller responded. "Let me look it up."

"We do have a box by that number. It is marked as confidential. I can't give you information for that number."

"But can you at least tell me if it belonged to my husband?"

"No. I'm sorry. We have strict rules."

"Then is there someone I can see here at the bank about it? I mean, if it belongs to my husband, then I should have access, because he's dead."

"I can't help you."

Rachel was getting a little exasperated. She just wanted to know if it belonged to him.

"Can I speak to a superior then?"

"Certainly. Please wait here."

Twenty minutes passed, and finally a heavyset balding man came out to talk to Rachel. He politely shook her hand and ushered her into his office.

"Mrs. Matthews, this is certainly a delicate situation. We have a box registered here to someone matching your husband's name. The box was leased four years ago, and it was paid in full for a period of five years. The lease isn't up yet, so that is probably why you have not been contacted about it."

"Well, I'm here. And Patrick is dead. So may I access the box?"

"No."

"Are you kidding?" she asked in dismay.

"We have a contract with strict orders to not allow anyone else to have access to this box. However, since you are saying he has passed away, and please accept my apologies, then we can make an exception for the person who has a notarized power of attorney."

"I'm the executor of his will. Does that count?"

"May I see a copy of his death certificate?"

"I don't have it with me."

"We need the certificate to confirm the information you are giving us, and we need to see the power of attorney."

"This is unbelievable. He is *dead*. And I am, or was, his wife."

"Ma'am, I'm not trying to be difficult, but if you bring us the notarized power of attorney, or a court order, then we can allow you access. And the death certificate."

"Okay," she exhaled deeply. "But you are confirming he has a box here, correct? Because I'm not going to go through all of this and then find out it was for nothing."

The vice-president of the bank just looked at her.

Rachel stood and walked out.

TWO DAYS LATER, Rachel returned with the documentation the bank's vice-president had requested and with her key to the mysterious box her husband had apparently leased.

A bank manager escorted her into a large chamber where a transparent bullet-proof door closed behind them. The banker looked for the shelf location of the box, inserted his guard key into the slot, and then asked Rachel to insert her key. A small door for the shelf was unlocked, and the banker removed a long metal box and set it on a table. He then removed the guard key from the shelf door, leaving Rachel's key in the lock until the box would be replaced and locked into place. The banker left the room closing the transparent door behind him.

Rachel was impressed with the integrity by which this bank protected its clientele's belongings, even though it had been a frustrating process to access the box originally.

She sat at the table for a few minutes before opening Patrick's box. What could he be hiding inside? Would it be something personal? Something secret? Why would he have leased the box four years ago and paid for a five-year contract? She had wondered for several days about the secrets the box would contain, and now she was faced with opening this very private part of Patrick's life. She brushed her hands across the cold metal box, knowing Patrick had been the last person to touch it.

God, please don't let me find out he was a spy against our country; or an embezzler or a jewel thief. If he had a double identity and was married to another family, I don't want to know.

No more conjecture. She opened the box.

It looked innocent enough. She looked down at the papers in the box and lifted the top one. It was a receipt from a jewelry store. She looked at it more carefully and read what it said.

2 Open Heart Necklaces @$98 each, w/tax = $205.80.

Two open heart necklaces? Like the one Patrick gave me for Christmas? That doesn't make any sense. Why would he buy two of them?

She set the receipt aside and looked at the papers remaining in the box. They were letters. She took them out, one by one, and looked at the envelopes. They had all been addressed to Patrick in a female's handwritten script. No man would write like that. There were no names or return addresses on them.

This isn't what I think it is.

Her heart was pounding loudly and her palms were sweaty as she slowly pulled one letter out of its envelope. The date indicated it had been written the week prior to Patrick's fatal trip to Bahrain. She began reading the letter…

My dearest Patrick,

I am so anxious to see you, my love! By next week I will be melting once again in your arms and feeling your body inside of mine. I miss you so much, even when you are just a few feet away. I can't bear seeing you across the room every day knowing you want me as much as I want you. We have to talk about this. The pain of being apart is becoming unbearable. I don't want you to be with her anymore, even if you have promised me I am the woman of your dreams. I anticipate this trip with every ounce of my being.

Lovingly yours.

Rachel was breathing heavily as thoughts swirling in her head flashed as headlines she could see but couldn't understand. She felt a sudden pain in her chest, as if an elephant was standing on top of her.

These letters couldn't belong to Patrick!

She threw the first letter aside and frantically opened the next one in the pile.

It was more of the same. There was talk about love and a future. There were occasional romantic poems and references to past interludes. There were also pages ripped out of magazines showing houses for sale near the beach.

Who wrote these letters? Was Patrick guarding them for a friend of his who was having an affair?

As she took the remaining letters out of the box, a photograph dropped from the pile onto the table. It was a picture of a woman scantily dressed in a negligée who was astutely hiding her face from the camera. Around her neck she wore a small brass key with an open heart.

Rachel inhaled deeply as she slowly picked up the photo from the table and gazed at the trinket around the woman's neck. She closed her eyes. After a moment, she looked at the photo again and examined it closely to make sure her mind wasn't playing tricks on her.

There is a second key?

She picked up the receipt she had found when she had first opened the box. It confirmed there were two keys. She felt the tears begin to escape from her eyes.

She looked at the woman for any identifying marks; anything that would indicate who had been having a love affair with her husband. She recognized nothing. She sorted through the letters for suggestions, but none of them identified the author. There were no return addresses anywhere.

Rachel finally acknowledged the letters had been intended for her husband. He had reciprocated the woman's feelings in the missives by giving her the second key to his heart.

She thought back to the last year of her marriage to Patrick. He had spent long hours at work, had increased his trips abroad, and his moodiness and isolation had been amplified around the family. He had made excuses for his irritability by telling her his job had become more complicated; that his new boss had expected more from him. Rachel remembered meeting his new boss, and while she agreed he was more demanding than the previous one, she knew the demands of Patrick's job couldn't have had anything to do with his decision to have an affair. Talking about the intensity of his work had most likely served as his cover when he had come home feeling guilty after spending hours at a rendezvous with his lover instead of time with his wife and children.

Rachel slowly realized she was sitting in the cold locked room of the bank's vault. She felt dizzy. She looked around her to see if the walls were actually closing in on her, or if it was only her imagination. She felt as if she couldn't breathe. She needed air. She had to get out of there. She had to go home and up to her room where all of this would go away.

She looked for a trash can where she could throw away the letters. There was none in the small room. She didn't want to touch them anymore, because that woman had touched them as she had written them, and Patrick had most certainly smiled and longed for her as he had read them.

How disgusting! How could you have deceived me,

Patrick?! And your children?

She wasn't sure if she had said that aloud or not, but she knew she had to get out of there before she really did scream. She would have to take the letters with her. Maybe she would burn them when she got home so no one would find out about them. It would be a secret, and she would protect Patrick's name for the sake of the children.

But what about *her*? How was *she* supposed to deal with this truth that changed everything she had ever believed to be real? Should she tell Darlene, or Erin? To what purpose? Maybe she'd tell her parents so she could get some comfort and reassurance from them. What about *his* parents? How would they feel if they knew what their son had done?

She picked up the letters to put them into her purse and suddenly felt sick.

These letters were written by a woman who had sex with my husband. She was naked with him. They shared intimate moments. What did he tell her about me while they were in bed? Did she laugh at me? Pity me? Did he make promises to her like he had made to me the night before he left?

She couldn't put the letters in her purse. They were filthy. They were full of deceits. She didn't want them touching her life inside her purse.

She walked over to the translucent door of the vault and knocked on it to get someone's attention.

"Yes, Mrs. Matthews. Are you ready for us to lock the box with you?"

"No. I will be closing this account. My husband is dead, and it was his account," Rachel responded to the gentleman. She then realized she had emphasized the word *dead* when she had spoken to him.

"Certainly. I'll get the vice-president and he will confirm you are closing the account. Is there anything else we can do for you today?"

"Yes. Do you have a plastic bag?"

The man looked at her confused and she pointed to the table inside the room. "I forgot to bring a bag for these papers."

"Oh, of course. One moment, please."

Secrets. Unsolicited choices and unwanted liabilities. Why did I have to find this key?

Chapter 15

RACHEL LEFT THE bank and pulled into her driveway at around five o'clock. The boys had called earlier asking permission to go next door to a friend's house to play video games.

She turned the key in the door and stepped inside her house. She stood in the foyer for a moment and looked around.

What was it that lured him away from his life here? From his children? From me?

She took a few steps and looked into the living room to her left. There was the plush blue couch they had purchased together after searching in thousands of furniture stores for the one that beckoned them, or so it had seemed. It had been their first major purchase for the new house before the boys were born. They had been sleeping on a mattress on the floor in the bedroom at the time, but they had made love on that couch the day it was delivered. Patrick had brought home a bottle of wine and they had decided to break in the couch that very evening.

She waked into the dining room beyond and ran her hands across the smooth oak table. She had wanted six chairs for the set, *just in case we have three or four children*, she recalled telling Patrick. At the time, he had been amenable to having a big family. After the twins were born, however, he had asked her to wait a couple of years before trying for a little girl. The years of waiting had slipped by as the details of their lives grew to ever so many. It seemed there had never been a perfect time to add to the family. As she stood by the table with the six empty chairs, something he had said suddenly made sense. She remembered a year before his death, when the boys were about nine, Patrick had come home and had said he wanted to get a vasectomy. He had told her it would be his gift to her. *Why*, she had asked. He had said they would be able to enjoy their lovemaking much more if they weren't always worrying about protection. But Rachel had *wanted* to get pregnant again. Patrick had been annoyed by her protestation, but he had agreed to delay the decision for another year and to talk about another baby during that time. That time never came. That is, until the night before he had gone to Bahrain. Rachel lowered her head as she fell into one of the chairs and her tears fell onto the table.

Suddenly she hit the unforgiving wood with all her strength creating a loud thud and rattling the porcelain tray in the center of it.

That was it, right? You wanted a vasectomy so you could have sex with your fucking girlfriend, right? It wasn't for me, was it? Is that why you didn't want another baby? Because you planned on leaving us, and you didn't want to leave another child behind for the courts to have to decide her fate? Did you even think about your sons while you were screwing your girlfriend?!

She wondered if Patrick and this woman had ever come to the house while she had been at work and the boys had been at school. Where else would they have gone? A hotel? She thought hard and tried to recall if there had ever been any signs of the bitch in her house. Perhaps a wine bottle missing from the pantry, or a second wine glass in the dishwasher. Maybe a wet towel in the bathroom that she had not questioned when she had come home from work. Had they showered here together? Maybe she should have agreed to take more showers with her husband. *But the stall was so small for two people*, she had always told him.

Surely he wouldn't have brought the woman to their home?

Rachel knew she would never have the answers to her questions. Patrick was dead. Her queries would haunt her throughout her days and would define her actions. She was sure the next man wouldn't stand a chance to her scrutiny; she would likely destroy the prospect of any healthy relationship before she was aware of what she was doing. *Could she truly leave this episode behind, and clear the tab for the next man in her life?* She wasn't sure she could. Two men had already cheated on her. Hadn't Michael done the same thing—cheated? Maybe that was too harsh of a term in his case. After all, he had appeared to be involved with Tyra Milano before he had met her. But he had withheld the truth about the other woman, hadn't he?

She hoped she would not dissect her own persona to a degree that no man could ever get through the front door. It would be easy to berate herself, to ask if she had been the cause of her husband's wanderings. *Was* she good enough for anyone else?

What did this other woman have that I didn't?!

Rachel wished she could confront Patrick and ask who the other woman had been. She wanted to know if he had loved the woman, or if he had just wanted her for sex. Could she have competed with someone who Patrick had fallen in love with? Would she have wanted to reclaim his love? And if she had regained his attention and fidelity, would she have always wondered if Patrick was thinking about the other woman while in bed with her?

If he hadn't loved the woman, maybe she could have forgiven her husband for his indiscretions. Surely it would have taken time and determination to recommit to the relationship and to trust and believe in each other. But it would have been possible, right? In spite of everything, she had loved him.

She felt the hurt grip her from deep inside. She wondered if he had really been thinking about getting a divorce, and if forgiveness would have been a moot point. Had he been slowly distancing himself from her so as to soften the blow when the time came to ask for the divorce?

What about his parents? Did they know anything? *No, surely they didn't*, she thought. He adored his parents. This would have killed them to know their son had cheated on his family. But if he *had* been planning a divorce, how would he have told his parents? Would he have left that up to her to tell them? Of course he would have, *the coward*. And now, is she supposed to tell them what she found out? About all the filthy letters of his tryst with some unidentified woman? No, she decided, it wasn't the time to make a rash decision like calling his parents. She still didn't even know who the woman was.

Oh, shit! What about friends? Did our friends know? His and mine?

Eric had been one of his best friends. Had he known what was going on? Did he try to stop Patrick from having the affair, or was he supportive of the tête-à-tête? Why would he have been sympathetic? Loyalty between men? Because he himself may have been having an affair? Did they all have affairs over there at Langley?

I can't even ask Eric, God, because he's dead too!

She sat there for a moment thinking about Eric and Dorothy and their longtime alliance. No, surely Eric didn't know, Rachel concluded, as she ran both hands through her hair and down her face. Eric was a family friend. He never would have condoned Patrick's behavior.

I'm sorry, God, for what I said about Langley. They're good guys. Eric was good. I just don't know what to think anymore. Please help me sort it out.

The tears started to run down her cheeks again, so she walked into the kitchen to find some tissues.

Rachel knew affairs happened all the time in real life, but they always happened to others. You always heard about it in the tabloids or through the grapevines in the community or at work.

She thought about her yoga instructor several years back who had been rumored to be having an affair with one of the men in their class, and both of them had been married at the time. They were fabulous people and well-respected in the community. Rachel remembered how the instructor had suddenly been replaced by another one, and the male client had dropped out of the class. Although it had been evident as to what had happened, no one had said a word about it. Apparently they had both asked for divorces, but then six months later, the instructor had gone back to her husband.

Why do affairs happen, God? Why don't marriages last anymore?

She remembered reading an article that reported more than half of the marriages in the United States end in divorce each year. *Why?* Aren't people strong enough in their convictions? Don't they have enough courage to stick to their vows and their beliefs? Or are beliefs becoming so elusive that people don't know what is right or wrong anymore? Is there some grey area where it is okay to have an affair if no one knows, or as long as no one is hurt?

Life is not easy. There are children to raise, mortgages to pay, bosses to please, and chores nagging at you and eating up the free moments that could be spent together as a couple. Rachel looked at the calendar on her refrigerator. It was full of errands and *gottas*; got to do this and got to do that. Really? Not one day said *HAVE FUN* on it. Not *one*.

What kind of life did I create for Patrick? Was it that bad living with me? I can be fun! Didn't he know that?

She took the calendar down and threw it violently in the trash. She paced around for a moment in the kitchen and then took it out of the trash again.

She thought about what a typical day had been in their lives the last year before Patrick's death. She would come home from work in time to meet the boys after they had finished school. Since she worked at a high school, her release time was earlier than theirs. She'd sit with the boys as they did their homework, and she would grade some papers. Then she'd start dinner. Patrick would come home at about six and would go up to change. He'd come back down and sit in the kitchen to look through the mail and read the newspaper. Then she'd put dinner on the table and call the boys in. They'd all talk about their day. After dinner, Patrick would wash the dishes and Rachel would put the leftovers away and make lunches for the next day. The boys would go up for showers. Patrick would go downstairs to the computer or to watch the news on TV. He was a multi-tasker, and often did both. Rachel would get everyone's clothes together for the next day and make sure all the baseball gear was washed and put back in the baseball bags. Then she'd grade some more papers while watching television with Patrick and the boys. By nine o'clock they'd usher the boys upstairs for bed, and after tucking them in, even at the age of eight or nine, Rachel would stay upstairs and read a book with them. Patrick would go back downstairs for some more TV or to work on the computer. And that was it. Unless, of course, there was a baseball game or basketball game to attend, or some other school or athletic event. That would be a whole different scenario.

Certainly there had been fun times too, hadn't there? The routine wasn't everything. Every couple of weeks she had gone with Patrick to the neighbor's house for a happy hour or dinner, or to Eric and Dorothy's house with the military gang. They had gone to movies and bike rides in the park with the kids on the weekends. And putt-putt golf. Oh, and to the neighborhood pool every weekend in the summers. They had also gone bowling on many Fridays with their adult friends and their kids, and to the Pizza Hut afterwards. Sometimes they'd just sit out on the deck for dinner with a glass of wine and assurances to have sex after the boys went to sleep. Wasn't all of that how it was supposed to be? It was a full life, wasn't it? There was no emptiness; no need for anything more. Hadn't Patrick felt that way? Had she misjudged him and his desire for more than what they had? What *did* he want? Money? Excitement? Travel? The thrill of endangerment or risk? Was the stability of the family too ordinary for him?

Who was this man I married?

She wondered if Patrick had been a reckless person and had been unconcerned about anyone other than himself when he had initiated the affair. Or had the affair been something he had just stumbled into, unaware of what was happening until it was too late? Maybe the woman had seduced him while his mind was unaware of how his body was responding. He had always thought things through. He was so meticulous. His job required that of him. But it also required a combination of that trait with a penchant for uncertainty and daring exploration. So were his eyes wide open? Did he know what he was doing?

This woman had changed everything for Rachel and her family.

Did the bitch even consider that? Did she even think about Patrick's sons?

Rachel wondered if the other woman had been married. Did the woman have children of her own? Had she planned to wreck her own family as well as Patrick's?

She knew in her heart the affair couldn't have been one-sided; it couldn't have been all on the woman. Patrick had not been stupid. After all, he had leased a safe deposit box for the letters he had received. He hadn't thrown the letters away or burned them, and there had had to be a reason. He had loved the other woman. He had wanted to keep her words near his heart. He had wanted to read her letters over and over and relive their moments together.

Rachel walked back out into the foyer and looked at Patrick's picture hanging on the wall. The thought of him loving the other woman left her breathless, and she fell to the carpet on her knees holding her wounded heart, rocking back and forth as she sobbed.

What did you do to us, Patrick?

I loved you. I still do. You were my everything. I know you were just human and that temptation comes to everyone. I just wish I had been enough for you, or that you would have at least told me you were having doubts. I would have fixed it. I would have done better as a wife.

God, what am I going to do now?

She sat there on the floor for a while and then realized the boys would be coming home soon. She knew Patrick had loved his sons, and the affair had not been about them.

She lifted herself off the floor and carefully took the picture of Patrick off the wall where it was hanging in the foyer. She couldn't see him anymore. It wasn't the same man. All the emotions his image evoked were changing so quickly. She saw his smile, but suddenly it was no longer warm and honest and loving.

She threw the picture frame against the wall and glass shards scattered across the floor. She stepped on the pieces of glass and heard them crunch under her shoes as she made her way to the stairs and went up to her bedroom.

She dropped her purse on the floor, walked over to the warm cozy chair in the corner of her bedroom, and curled up in it. She became aware that Oliver was staring up at her and was concerned about his master. He had probably been beside her the whole time, but she had been too absorbed to notice. She slipped out of the chair and onto the floor and petted his head. Then the anguish and tears came in floods. She grabbed the afghan off the back of the chair and wrapped herself up in it. She hugged her dog tightly as he lay there with his head nuzzled in her neck. She felt safe with Oliver. He was loyal. If the other woman had come into the house, Oliver would have barked incessantly at her. Oliver had always protected Rachel and the kids; no one could ever come through the front door without Oliver's scrutiny and approval. Yes, he would have bitten the woman's head off.

"MOM?" BRANDON CALLED from the stairs below. "Is everything okay here?"

Brandon and Andrew had come home for dinner, as expected, at six o'clock. Rachel had fallen asleep for the past half hour on her bedroom floor, but she awoke to the sound of Oliver running down the stairs to greet the boys.

"Mom? Dad's picture is broken and there's glass all over the floor!" Brandon called up to his mom as he held the photograph of his father in his hands and gingerly walked around the broken glass in the foyer.

"Mom!" Andrew yelled when he heard no response.

"Yes! Yes," Rachel responded finally, "I'm up here. I'm just changing from work and I'll be down in one minute!"

She quickly changed into a t-shirt and jeans and turned to go downstairs. She saw the letters in the plastic bag on the floor beside her purse, and she threw the bag under her bed.

"Here I am!" she said coming down the stairs composed as if nothing had intruded on their lives.

Brandon was holding the picture of his father in his hands, and Andrew had gone to the kitchen to find a broom to sweep up the glass.

"What happened here?" Andrew asked his mom as he came back into the hallway with the broom.

"Oh, the picture. I'm so sorry, guys. I came in with some big shopping bags, and I hit the picture accidentally with my elbow and it fell off the wall. I was just changing clothes and then I was going to sweep it up," she responded quickly. "Here, give me the boom, Andrew."

"Why is the glass all the way over here if it just fell off the wall?" Andrew's tone was concerned. She knew he didn't buy her story.

She sighed and no one said anything for a moment.

"Come here, guys," she said. "Let's go sit down in the living room for a minute."

What do you say to your children when you have just found out their father cheated on his family? But had he *really* cheated on the boys, or was this just about her? Should she tell them their father had slept with another woman, had carried on a double life, and had secretly hidden letters in a safe deposit box? Should they know he was probably with the other woman when he was gone on his trips the last year of his life? That he had probably missed their baseball games and the trip to Washington for spring break, because of the other woman? That the other woman meant more to their father than her?

She wondered if by telling them the truth, they would blame her for his alienation from the family. They loved their father, and she knew they loved her, but they could not ask him why he had abandoned them. So they would have to ask *her* the questions, for which she had no answers. Would they attribute their father's distancing to their mother's shortcomings? Or ask if they had had a fight before he left, causing him to be inattentive on the road, resulting in his accident and death?

Oh my God! Had that been it? Did I cause the accident?

"What is it, mom?" Brandon asked.

"Okay, I'm going to be honest, but just understand that grown-ups sometimes make poor decisions, and the reasons are complicated. You will understand more when you are older, but right now you just have to trust me, okay?" She searched for the words.

"Since your father died," she continued, "it has been tough on all of us, and we have all missed him a lot. Right?"

"Right," Andrew answered, "but we're okay, mom. Aren't you?"

"Well, yes. And no. Some days I wake up very strong and willing to face anything that comes at me. Other days, not so much. Some days I feel almost happy again, and other days I feel guilty about feeling happy as if nothing had happened."

"So why did you break his picture, mom?"

There it was. They knew she had broken it purposefully.

"Today was one of those confusing days when I was just angry. It's hard to handle a tough situation without a partner to help you through things, you know?"

"So you were mad because dad wasn't here to help you?"

"I think so. I had a lot of questions I couldn't answer, and I guess I was a bit angry he wasn't here to answer them for me."

"What questions?"

"It's complicated. But nothing for you to worry about. We all love each other, and I know you loved your dad very much." She grabbed them and hugged them. "And I'm sorry I took it out on the glass frame and threw it on the wall. I'll replace it; I promise."

"That's okay, mom. You've always told us if we get angry, we shouldn't hit anyone, we should just throw something against a wall or punch a pillow."

They all looked at each other and laughed.

"Yes, I guess I did tell you that, didn't I?"

She hugged them again.

"But I'm sorry," she said again.

"Are you okay now?" Andrew asked.

"I'm okay," she reassured him with a smile.

And she was.

Chapter 16

WEEKS LATER, AFTER sifting through her emotions and coming out on the other side, Rachel decided to tell Darlene about Patrick's affair. Women need their friends. And this wasn't something she wanted to go through on her own, even if she did feel she had it under control.

Maybe Darlene could see things Rachel had not been able to see, especially from her counseling point of view. But she would only tell Darlene; no one else. Telling Darlene was like locking a secret in a vault and throwing away the key; unlike Patrick, who had kept the key on his key ring.

Rachel had decided not to tell the boys. If they were to find out someday and be upset with her for withholding the truth, so be it. She wanted to safeguard their childhood memories and their impressions as they navigated their future. She wanted them to have faith in humanity. She knew they still said little prayers to their dad at night and before their baseball games for good luck, and they probably asked for his guidance when they were making decisions only a dad could understand. He had been a hero to them. Why did that have to be destroyed? Patrick *was* a hero. His work had been invaluable to the military, as the Lieutenant General had eloquently written in his letter to the family when Patrick had died. No, it was best not to disclose anything to them for now.

Rachel remembered studying two French philosophers in college: Voltaire and Rousseau. The two had debated a similar query. Is it better to know the truth and possibly be devastated by that knowledge? To be condemned to a life of caution and suspicion of others? Or is it best to live in a world believing everyone is innately virtuous and guiltless? To be able to give every new acquaintance a clean slate with which to earn loyalty and trust? Rachel had decided to embrace the philosophy espoused by Rousseau and keep the truth to herself so that others would not suffer. And yet, she still wanted to know who the woman had been who had stolen her husband, even at the price of desolation. Didn't she have the right to know?

Darlene had used her best counseling skills and had advised Rachel against doing anything drastic.

"You're angry right now, Rach. And that is totally normal. But beating yourself up about the reasons for Patrick's indiscretions, and trying to find out who the other woman is, will not help you. You need to move on. His issues are not your problems, so drop them."

"How can you say that? They *are* my problems, Darlene. Don't you see? If he pulled away from me, it was for a reason. If I ever fall in love again, and that's a big *if*, then I don't want to make the same mistakes that will push someone else away."

"Okay, that makes sense. But I don't think you will ever really know what pulled him away from you. It may have been a one-time thing; he may have simply been tired one night and given in to temptation. And then maybe he didn't know how to end the whole thing."

"I don't think so. The letters from the woman clearly responded to things he had said in his letters to her. He was definitely in this for the distance. I just don't understand what drove him there and kept him there."

"We don't always get our answers, Rachel. But trying to change yourself to become someone else that another man would desire is not the answer. You are you, and you are wonderful the way you are. That's what attracted Patrick in the first place."

"Then why did he throw me away?"

"I don't know. But I do know you can't stop being who you are. You can't live some other Rachel's life. You need to be true to yourself. If some guy doesn't like this Rachel, then screw him. You don't need him. There is someone out there that wants *this* Rachel. I know it. You just need to give it time."

"But I'm so afraid I will choose the wrong man again. I'm too trusting and naive. I mean, look at what happened to me this past Christmas when I was at Lake Placid!"

"That guy loved you, Rachel. And I don't believe you really know the full extent of his story."

"That he was sleeping with two women at the same time? It couldn't have been any clearer than that." She paused for a moment. "And why are you always defending Michael and Patrick by trying to justify what they did?"

"I'm not defending them. I'm on your side. But there are always two sides to a story, Rachel. You know that."

"I know," she sighed. "But they hurt me. I'm not so

sure I can forgive either one of them."

"You're not being fair."

"Yes I am."

"No, you're not. You're angry at Patrick and you're taking it out on Michael."

"Why are we even talking about him? What does Michael have to do with all of this?"

"Erin and I feel like you should try to contact Michael and talk about what happened to you two at Lake Placid."

"Why?"

"Because you should give the guy a chance."

"Wait, you talked to my sister-in-law about this?"

"Yes," Darlene said cautiously. "Look, Erin has been concerned about you. When she came down here to help while Andrew was in the hospital, we talked. She told me all about Michael, from her perspective, not yours."

"I can't believe you two talked about me."

"Don't you go making this about a trust issue, Rachel. These are two friends talking about their best friend, okay? We love you and we care."

"Okay, you're right. What did she say about Michael? I mean, what was her take on it?"

"She watched you two fall in love in front of her eyes. And yes, it's possible to fall in love that quickly, okay?"

Darlene could always read her friend's mind.

"It *was* quick," Rachel responded. "That doesn't make me a freak, does it?"

"No, you goofball."

"What else did she say?"

"Erin said Michael was an honest and caring person. She told me he fell in love with the boys, too, and it wasn't artificial; it was real."

"So?"

"So I think you read too much into this Tyra lady when she kissed him. A lot of friends kiss on the mouth, Rach. I mean, guys to ladies and ladies to men," she corrected herself. "Oh what the hell—you get what I mean!"

"What about him sleeping with her?"

"Did he say he was sleeping with her *now*, or did he say he *slept* with her?"

"Those are semantics! Are we really going to go there, Darlene?"

"Okay, girl, calm down! So what if he did sleep with her a long time ago, and it didn't work out, but they are still friends. He didn't marry her, right?"

"I don't know."

"You don't know if he married her?"

"No, I mean, I don't know if it would matter to me if he had slept with her a long time ago. I guess men can't be celibate forever."

"I can't believe I'm hearing you say that."

"What?"

"Look, you slept with him when you were at Lake Placid, right? So how is that any different than him sleeping with her years ago?"

"Because we loved each other?"

"Don't be so old-fashioned, Rachel. People sleep together, okay? Sex is healthy. It's fun. And people find partners to sleep with even if they don't love each other."

"Okay, so now we're talking about morals."

"I'm not saying that Michael was sleeping around, Rach. I'm just saying that a man can't go for twenty years without sex just because he hasn't found the right woman to marry, okay?"

"Okay," she conceded. "That makes sense."

Darlene gave her a look.

"No, that does make sense, Darlene. I guess I'm really old-fashioned, aren't I?"

"I didn't say it, you did!"

Chapter 17

RACHEL FELT STRONGER as the weeks passed following her discovery at the bank. She had promised Darlene
she would try to put the whole affair in the past and move
on. And yet, she knew if she didn't try to find out who the
other woman had been in Patrick's life, it would become a
nagging drone in the distance. It would always follow her,
waiting to attack her when she was most vulnerable. She
would wonder if the lady next to her in the grocery store
had been his lover. Or maybe it had been the veterinarian
where they took Oliver for his check-ups. Or perhaps it had
been their financial advisor with her long black shiny hair.
In any case, she had decided to discreetly investigate her
husband's lover. She would decide whether or not to confront the woman based on what she found out about her.

Rachel read the letters again over the next couple of
days. She was looking for hints; something that could help
her figure out who the other woman had been. She also
thought about the weeks before the accident and jotted
down some notes about what she could remember. Then
she went through the accident report she had received from
the Air Force after Patrick's funeral.

As she set the letters and documents aside to study her notes, something was tugging at the back of her mind; something she remembered reading in the last letter the woman had written to her husband. What had the letter said?

I miss you so much, even when you are just a few feet away. I can't bear seeing you across the room every day knowing you want me as much as I want you.

Across the room? The woman had seen Patrick every day across the room. The office. It had to have been someone who worked with him at Langley.

Chapter 18

ON A FRIDAY evening after the boys had been picked up by their grandparents for the weekend, Rachel drove to the house of her estranged friend, Dorothy. She had called her in advance, and Dorothy had been amenable to seeing her. She expected the visit would be a bit awkward at first, as the two military wives hadn't seen each other for nearly two years. Their separation hadn't been a deliberate or immediate alienation; rather a gradual progression following the event that took their husbands' lives. Perhaps each one had been a painful reminder to the other of what had occurred.

On her way there, Rachel ruminated about the other military wives she had leaned on for support when she had been so miserable and hopeless. The ladies had selflessly devoted their time and assistance to her and Dorothy following the demise of their husbands in Bahrain. They had run errands for them, had offered to take care of Brandon and Andrew when needed, had walked and fed Oliver, and their husbands had assisted Dorothy and Rachel with yard work. That's what the military did; they stuck together and helped their own.

Eventually, however, the friends' efforts at consolation had turned into an increasingly uncomfortable ritual of questions-and-answers each time the group got together. *Are you okay? Are you sure? Are you seeing a therapist? Are the boys seeing one? Are you managing okay at home alone? Do you need any help? How is the lawsuit going? Did you meet the truck driver in court? What did the witnesses say?* It just went on and on, and it became too disheartening to endure. Rachel had sought out the group of friends as a distractor from her hardships, not as a dismal reminder. They had all meant well, but Rachel had known she would have to distance herself from the group if she had wanted to heal; and so she did.

In due course, she reflected, the remainder of the group had separated as well. The outings to movies and restaurants had become less frequent. Rhonda and a few of the others had attached themselves to a new group of military wives, and Rachel rarely saw them other than an occasional awkward sighting at the commissary. Jaclyn had transferred to an Air Force base in Maryland, and Dorothy had disassociated herself from the group to spend more time at her family's beach house on the eastern shore of Virginia.

In any case, here she was. She had arrived at Dorothy's house at five-thirty but was still sitting in her car rehearsing the questions she had planned to ask. As she sat there summoning her courage to confront Dorothy, she saw someone across the street look out of a window from behind the curtains. *Time to go*, she decided, or some neighbor might mistake her for a stalker.

She got out of the car and walked slowly towards the house. She stood on the doorstep for a moment, and without notice, Dorothy opened the door.

Both women exchanged pleasantries, and Dorothy invited Rachel into the living room to sit and talk. Rachel decided to get right to the point.

"Who was sitting beside Patrick in the car, Dorothy?"

"What do you mean?" She was instantly caught off guard.

"I think you know," Rachel persisted. "Patrick and Eric were hit broadside, meaning Eric was in the back seat behind Patrick. Why wasn't he in the front?"

There was silence. Dorothy was staring at the floor.

Rachel sat forward on the sofa and leaned towards Dorothy's chair nearby.

"Why wasn't Eric in the front?" she repeated.

"Rachel, I can't…"

"Tell me, Dorothy. Please."

There was more silence.

"You know then," Rachel said leaning back on the sofa. "Jaclyn was sitting in the front, not Eric, because she was having an affair with Patrick."

"Yes."

Dorothy looked down at her hands in her lap. Rachel looked at the bay window as the last rays of sunlight peeked through an opening in the curtains and cast shadows on the walls like dead soldiers looming and waiting for their consequence.

"Rach, I…"

"Don't call me *Rach*! Only my close friends call me that!"

She looked away with tears in her eyes. It had been confirmed. Patrick had been having an affair with Jaclyn.

How many other people knew? Was it true, then, the wife is always the last to know? Had people been pointing fingers at her all along and laughing? Mocking her and wondering what she had done to drive her husband away? Judging her whole life?

"Please, Rachel," Dorothy pleaded. "I didn't know she was going to be on that trip. Believe me. None of us did."

"*None of you*? How many people knew about her and Patrick, Dorothy?"

"I don't know," Dorothy's voice trailed off. "Eric and I suspected, but we weren't sure at the time."

"Then when *were* you sure, Dorothy? At your dinner party? After they went on that trip together? When Patrick had to kick Eric out of the room so he could sleep with his whore in Bahrain? Did Eric call and tell you all the sordid details?"

"Okay, *wait*, Rachel. *Stop* accusing me! I was your friend, and so was Eric. We were friends to you *and* Patrick. We didn't cause this, Rachel."

There was quiet as Dorothy looked at her accuser.

"What do you want from me?" Dorothy continued. "Do you want the details? Is that what you want from me?"

"Crap," Rachel responded under her breath when she realized she had been condemning Dorothy as an accomplice. It wasn't Dorothy's fault.

Why am I being so insensitive to this woman who also lost her husband? I'm such a bully!

"I'm sorry," Rachel said at last. "But yes, it would help if you could give me a little background, Dorothy. Whatever you feel comfortable sharing. I don't want to pressure you. I just think it would help me understand the situation, and then maybe I can stop beating myself up for being such a poor excuse of a wife."

"No, Rachel. You were *not* a bad wife, believe me." She got up from her chair and came over to the sofa and put her hand on Rachel's.

"Thank you..."

"Okay," Dorothy said as she slightly pulled away from her friend to begin her account, "I'll tell you what I know."

Dorothy described how she and Eric had deduced Patrick was having an affair. Patrick had told his friend he had had to go on an unexpected excursion to Saudi Arabia one month prior to the Bahrain trip. Eric had doubted there was a mission in Saudi Arabia, but they were in an intelligence and reconnaissance division, and not everyone knew what everyone else was doing at Langley, so it could have been plausible. In any case, Eric had noticed Jaclyn was gone from the unit at the same time Patrick had taken leave. She had claimed she was sick. Dorothy said she had called Jaclyn's home to offer assistance while she was sick, but Jaclyn's husband had said his wife had gone to her mother's house in Pennsylvania. Apparently she had told her husband Paul that she had needed to help with her mother's recovery after she had taken a fall. That had been their first inkling of their friend's affair.

Dorothy shared that Patrick hadn't been himself at the office after the Saudi Arabia trip; he had become mysterious and reclusive when Eric had tried to have conversations with him. Coincidentally, Eric had noticed an emerging attraction between his friend and Jaclyn. The electricity in the room had been obvious when they were together; there had been fleeting looks, a hand on Patrick's shoulder whenever she had spoken to him at his desk, and glances around the office to see if anyone had been listening to their whispers. Eric had also noticed Jaclyn and Patrick exchanging envelopes, but he hadn't been sure if the envelopes were work-related or personal.

Shortly thereafter, the unit had been assigned to Bahrain. No one had known about Jaclyn's intent to join the team overseas at the time. She had not mentioned it at the dinner party the night before the trip. Paul, her husband, hadn't even known. Nevertheless, Jaclyn had offered her unique expertise for the mission, and Langley had granted her request to connect with the team three days later. In retrospect, Dorothy surmised, Jaclyn had probably known all along she would be going to Bahrain. Patrick had most likely been cognizant as well.

Dorothy shared that Eric had confronted Patrick at their dinner party the night before the trip. He had pulled him aside and had told him about his suspicions regarding the rendezvous in Saudi Arabia. Patrick had disputed the allegations. Dorothy knew about this exchange because Eric had been upset and had told his wife about it after their party.

"Maybe that's why Patrick was so distressed when we came home that evening," Rachel shared. "We had a big argument that night."

"I know."

"What do you mean?"

Dorothy continued with her account. On the trip to Bahrain, she explained, Patrick unloaded his burden by confirming his friend's suspicions and admitting to his affair. The dispute between the two men the prior evening had apparently served as a wake-up call for him. Patrick shared that he and Rachel had reconciled and that he was determined to do whatever it would take to restore his marriage. He had decided to end the relationship with Jaclyn upon their arrival in Bahrain.

"How did you find out all of this? Did Eric tell you?"

"Yes. He called me several hours after landing in Bahrain to let me know he had arrived safely, and he told me about their talk. He had promised Patrick he'd keep their conversation private, and he asked me to do the same."

"I see."

"We didn't want to hurt anyone, Rachel. And Patrick needed to know he could trust Eric. We just wanted your marriage to have a chance to mend. We figured it was Patrick's prerogative to handle the issue the way he felt best."

"I guess. I'm not sure."

"Everyone should have second chances," Dorothy said, "even Patrick."

Rachel knew Dorothy truly believed what she was saying. She could not blame her for having kept the information a secret from her; as long as she hadn't shared it with anyone else.

"Did Eric tell you anything else in subsequent phone calls from Bahrain?"

"Are you sure you want to know?"

"Yes."

Dorothy took a few moments to collect her thoughts, and then she shared what she could remember from the conversations with her husband while he was overseas. She recalled hearing Jaclyn had not accepted the news well when Patrick had ended their affair. As a matter of fact,

Eric had reported, she had become increasingly agitated and unpredictable during the days remaining of their mission abroad. So much so, the other team members had noticed the change in her demeanor and had started asking questions. Eric had tried to stay out of it as much as possible and had feigned ignorance so as not to betray his friend's confidence. Patrick, however, had worried Jaclyn would do something irrational, even though he had not been quite sure what it would be. The more he had tried to apologize and calm her, the more inconsolable she had become. At that point, he had decided to avoid her, hoping the distance between them would help her recover enough to finish the mission in Bahrain with dignity. Evading her had made the situation worse. Patrick had shared with Eric that Jaclyn had continued to follow him around the base incessantly pleading for him to reconsider his decision; but he had remained resolute. She had tried to corner him whenever he was alone, and had tried to visit him in his room at night. He had been glad Eric was his roommate.

Two nights later, the evening before they had been expected to return to the United States, several members of the team had decided to leave the base and go to a restaurant to celebrate their successful mission. Patrick had been certain Jaclyn would insist on riding in his car, so he had asked Eric in advance to ride with them. He had not wanted to be alone with Jaclyn for fear he would say something that could be misconstrued and thus perpetuate her hope for a future together. He had figured Eric's presence in the car would give him a respite from the arguing as well. Surely Jaclyn wouldn't want Eric or anyone else to know about their indiscretions.

"Do you know what happened the night of the accident?"

"No one knows, Rachel. The last call I had from Eric was the one right before they left the base for the restaurant."

"Do you think Jaclyn and Patrick were arguing, causing him to lose control of the car?"

"No one could ever know if Patrick would have been more alert on the road had he not been distracted by his concern for Jaclyn, Rachel. But I think it was unlikely."

"Do you blame Patrick for Eric's death?"

"No. The officers in the car behind them confirmed the truck driver had recklessly sped through the red light after Patrick had advanced through the green one."

They both sat there for a moment as stillness filled the room and questions hovered unanswered.

"Jaclyn survived. Did she ever tell you anything?" Rachel asked.

"No. As you know, she kind of distanced herself from all of us."

"Yes, I remember she didn't even attend Eric and Patrick's funerals at Arlington. Neither did her husband Paul. I guess I didn't give it much thought at the time."

"None of us did. I remember she later went to court as a witness in the litigation against the trucking company, but she didn't reveal anything we didn't already know."

"Do you think Paul knew about the affair? I mean, we didn't see much of either one of them after the accident."

"He figured it out in time. He probably thought there were other people in the group who knew, so that may have been why he detached himself from everyone."

"How do you think he found out?"

Dorothy explained that Paul had been suspicious after the Saudi Arabia trip when he had found out Jaclyn had not actually gone to Pennsylvania to help her mother. But he had accepted the excuse she had given him, which was her having to keep the operation in the Middle East a secret for security purposes. After she had been unexpectedly assigned to the Bahrain mission, however, his suspicions returned. He began to question her superiors at the base about her trips. They had been as surprised to hear his accusations as he had been to hear she had been the one to request the mission to Bahrain. He had become more wary when Jaclyn had refused to attend the funerals of her two fellow officers. She had become despondent, and she had languished around the house grieving for more than the loss of two friends. Paul instinctively knew it had to have been due to a woman's bereavement for the loss of a soul mate.

"How did you know all of this?"

"He told me. He came to my house asking questions just as you are here today."

"Oh. I guess he didn't feel comfortable coming to me in case I didn't know about the affair."

"Correct. He is a decent guy, Rachel, and he loved his wife as much as you loved Patrick. He would never want to see anyone harmed, I'm certain."

"Whatever happened to him and Jaclyn?"

"Paul and Jaclyn eventually decided to get a divorce. I figured he knew he could never measure up to the passion his wife had felt for Patrick, and he hadn't wanted to settle for less."

Rachel cringed at the last remark about Jaclyn's passion for Patrick.

It didn't go unnoticed.

"I'm sorry; I didn't mean to hurt you with that comment," Dorothy said.

"So they got divorced?"

"Yes. Jaclyn requested a transfer to the military base in Maryland. Paul stayed in Hampton where he was, and still is, working at an investment firm. People see him in town every now and then at a restaurant or at a movie by himself."

"I know it took a lot of courage for you to talk to Paul, and now me. I guess we felt you were the only person with answers, but I'm not even sure why."

"I don't have all the answers, Rachel. But I hope you find what you are looking for."

RACHEL LEFT DOROTHY'S house that evening feeling as if some of the pages of Patrick's secret life had been revealed to her. There were still more pages written in indelible ink, and she knew she'd continue in her search to expose them for a fuller understanding of who her husband had become those last few years of his life. Maybe she wouldn't be able to unearth all the pages, but perhaps enough of them to attain the closure she desired. She was getting there.

She had learned Patrick had ultimately chosen her over the other woman, and he had terminated the affair. That meant something. It meant he had truly loved her the night before his trip to Bahrain. It had not been a lie. And the baby they had conceived that night had been a result of their love and commitment to each other.

The information from Dorothy, however, didn't necessarily detract from Rachel wanting to know what had derailed her marriage in the first place. It couldn't have been all on Patrick; it had to have been partly her fault as well.

She also wondered if she would have fought to keep her marriage had she known about the affair. One can always predict what one would do in this case, either forgive and forget, or go for the divorce, but one never knows for sure until it becomes a reality. She'd never know.

Rachel knew, however, she would have to sort through all those questions and emotions prior to having a healthy relationship with any other man in the future. Perhaps that's why things hadn't worked out with Michael Blanford; maybe God had predicted she wouldn't have been ready for him under the current circumstances. How could she have maintained a new relationship while pursuing the truth about her husband's infidelity? While going through Andrew's illness and recovery? While living hundreds of miles away from California? And yet, there were times she couldn't stop thinking about the way she had felt when she had been in Michael's arms.

Chapter 19

THE DAY AFTER her visit to Dorothy, Rachel drove to Paul Rossman's house. She wasn't quite sure why she had felt the need to talk to him. Empathy? Affiliation? Perhaps Paul had already come to terms with the reasons for his failed marriage and had closed that chapter of his life. Did she really have the right to reopen it?

But she was here on his doorstep. Too late.

Why am I so impulsive at the expense of others?

Paul answered the door on the first knock. Disbelief registered on his face as he saw Rachel standing on his porch, but he managed a big smile. Rachel knew it had been a mistake to not call him in advance.

"Come in, Rachel. Are you okay?"

"Yes," she said, hugging him the way they had always done when the group had been intact.

"It's been a long time," he said sincerely. "What brings you here?"

"Do you mind if we sit for a few minutes?"

Rachel told Paul she had recently found out about the affair between his former wife and Patrick, and she told him she knew he had also found out about it years ago.

"Why didn't you ever tell me, Paul?" she asked gently, remembering how the harsher approach with Dorothy had created unwanted friction between them.

"What would have been the point, Rachel?"

"Weren't you angry? Didn't you want to expose the affair?" Her questions came spilling out too fast.

Calm down; remember he went through this too.

"I loved my wife, Rachel. And the fact she and I are divorced does not change how I feel for her now. I would have stayed with her, but she was too devastated after Patrick's death. That's when I understood I could not compete with a ghost, with his memory. I had to let her go."

Paul sat in silence for a few moments. It seemed as if there had been many moments of silence as of late.

"Rachel, I don't blame Patrick. I don't even blame Jaclyn. Affairs happen, and no one can explain why. Maybe I was too involved with work, too distant, so she responded to the attentions of another man." He fidgeted in his chair when he realized he had just insinuated Patrick had preyed on his wife.

Rachel understood. She waited for him to continue.

"Look," he said, "Jaclyn was always attracted to military men, and I wasn't one of them, so maybe she went after your husband when she got bored with me. I think she married me because I was stable. We had the same goals in life. We had wanted the house and picket fence and kids and a dog. But I was never the exhilarating adventurer Patrick was."

"And the house and dog weren't enough?"

"I guess not."

Her thoughts lingered for just a second, and then she

proceeded cautiously. "Why didn't you ever have kids? I mean, if you don't mind me asking."

She felt sorry for this man in front of her who was revealing his unrequited affection for his ex-wife. She didn't want to pry or hurt him with her questions. She just wanted to understand. But she knew she may have stepped over the line with her last question.

"She couldn't have children," he responded looking into the distance beyond Rachel.

That doesn't make sense, Rachel thought. Patrick had asked for a vasectomy. But maybe it had not been for Jaclyn, rather her. Maybe he hadn't wanted her to get pregnant making it more difficult to get a divorce later on.

"We didn't know about the infertility until a couple of years after we were married. In retrospect, it may have helped us if she could have been a mom. I should have encouraged her to adopt a child. But it's all water under the bridge now. It doesn't help to keep trying to analyze this whole thing and to beat ourselves up in the process."

He probably meant that to be a message for her, Rachel thought. Maybe he was trying to tell her he had already travelled this path three years ago, almost four now, and that there are no clear answers to the questions tormenting them both.

"Okay," Rachel said. "Okay."

She stood to leave and Paul stood as well. She gave him a hug, said good-bye, and left.

It helped to know someone else was in this boat with her, even though she knew they both felt culpable about each other's spouse's role in ending their respective marriages.

Chapter 20

RACHEL LOVED BASEBALL season. It was a Saturday, and Brandon and Andrew had just finished playing a rare game of one's team against the other's team. These infrequent games were always bittersweet because one team would win while the other team would lose. It was inevitable. One son would be frustrated while the other would be celebrating. The boys were always respectful of each other's feelings, however. The winner would commiserate with the brother whose team had lost and would offer encouraging words for the next game. The loser would come around and manage a smile and congratulations for his brother.

This time Andrew's team lost. But there wasn't anything some ice-cream couldn't cure.

Rachel had invited Darlene to join them in an after-game binge of ice cream sundaes at the local Friendly's restaurant. Actually, Darlene had been the one to call Rachel earlier in the day to see if she could meet her somewhere after the game. She had said she wanted to show her something. Rachel assumed it had something to do with the wedding coming up in three months.

Rachel was excited to share her own news: she had received a call from the Lotus Winery winemaker, Andreas, about the possibility of a job there in the summer. Andreas had asked her to come for an interview the following week.

"HI, RACHEL! HI, guys!" Darlene swooped in and sat down next to them in the restaurant. "I hate to ask, but whose team won the game today?"

"Brandon's," Andrew responded with just a slight tone of disappointment.

"Yeah, buddy!" she said raising her hand in the air to give Brandon a high-five. "And good fight, Andrew," she said turning to the other brother and high-fiving him as well.

"They were both stupendous today!" Rachel said. "Andrew had a fabulous line drive to left field and scored a double. He went three for four. And Brandon also had three for four."

"Don't forget his homerun!" Andrew interjected. "You should have seen him, he hit that sucker so hard it flew over the fence never to be seen again!"

"Yeah, everybody was going crazy!" Rachel said.

"Good job, guys," Darlene commended them again.

They all ordered their sundaes, and Brandon and Andrew went off to another table to join some teammates who had arrived around the same time. Friendly's was the unofficial hangout for the local baseball teams following their games, and the boys had enjoyed coming to meet up with their friends after the coaches let them go. There always seemed to be a good number of girls their age at the restaurant right around the same time, too. Coincidence?

"Hey, I have something to show you," Darlene finally said to Rachel.

"And I have something to tell you," Rachel responded.

"Okay, you go first, Rach. Mine can wait."

"I think I have a summer job at a winery!" she blurted out with delight.

"Are you kidding? Tell me about it!"

"Well, there's not too much to tell, yet. I got a call from the Lotus Winery today while I was at the baseball game." Rachel noticed that Darlene had a perplexed look on her face. "On my cell phone. I got the call on my cell phone."

"Oh! Gotcha. And...?"

"It was the winemaker, some guy named Andreas, and he said Elizabeth had given him my number and had told him I was interested in a job. He asked me a ton of questions, and I was honest about not having much experience, but I guess there was something I must have said that impressed him, because he asked me to come in for an interview next week. Isn't that great?!" She could barely contain her enthusiasm.

"Sure is! When is the interview?"

"He said Wednesday or Thursday. He's going to call me on Monday. The owners are out of town, but he said he and the other winemaker will both be there to meet with me."

"That's fabulous, Rachel. Just what you need."

"I really hope I get it, too. I am so nervous!"

"You'll do fine!" her friend assured her.

"I mean, how hard is it to pour wine? And I know a lot

about Virginia wines, so that's something, right? It won't take long to learn about their particular ones. I went online and looked at the list of wines from the former winery and memorized some stuff."

"Do you think the new owner will stick to the same kinds of wines the previous owners had? What is it called now, anyway?"

"I don't know the name, but I'll find out next week. And yes, they'll probably stick with some of the same wines at the beginning. It really takes about five years to get something new going. Maybe less. Unless they import grapes."

"I am so happy for you, Rach, really," Darlene said to her friend and took a bite of her ice-cream.

"So what is *your* news? What were you going to show me?" Rachel asked.

"Don't go getting all ballistic on me, okay?" she eyed her friend.

"What are you talking about?"

"Here," she said, taking a magazine out of her purse and sliding it across the table.

"A magazine?"

"You have to read it."

"I have to read a magazine. A magazine about movie stars and celebrities?" Rachel looked at her friend with a confused expression.

Darlene sighed. "Okay, I'll show you. But you don't have to read it now if you don't want to."

She turned some pages and came to the article she wanted her friend to read.

"Here, look at this," she said pointing to a photograph

of Tyra Milano.

"Darlene…"

"Come on! Read what it says under the photo."

"Tyra Milano comes out of the closet and announces her engagement to her partner of three years, Sherrie Gautier."

Rachel had read the words aloud. Then she read the caption again in silence to make sure she had read it correctly.

Darlene and Rachel looked at each other. Rachel's face registered confusion at first, and then astonishment.

"Are you kidding?" she finally said. "Tyra Milano is gay?"

"Yes ma'am."

"But she kissed Michael on the mouth that day at the ski lodge. And he said he had slept with her!"

"So if Tyra and this Sherrie person have been together for three years now, then Michael *wasn't* sleeping with her, Rach."

Rachel looked down at the photo of Tyra and Sherrie as her mind raced to the images of Michael kissing the celebrity in the lobby. Had she misinterpreted what she had seen?

"What exactly did he say to you when you asked him about Tyra, Rach?"

"He told me it was complicated and that he couldn't tell me any more about it."

"Then that's it. Tyra told him her secret and he wasn't about to give it up. He couldn't tell you she was gay and that she wasn't really with him."

"But she had a daughter!"

"Maybe it was her niece or someone else's daughter. Or maybe she had had a daughter in a previous relationship with a man, when she was still into men."

"Why wouldn't he have told me, Darlene?"

"Because he is an honorable man. He keeps people's secrets."

"God, I hate secrets!"

"Does this change anything? I mean, about how you feel about him?" her friend asked.

"No. He said he had sex with her. And furthermore, he misrepresented who she was by covering for her with all those photographers that day. He could have told me."

"Really, Rachel? She was his *friend*, and friends protect friends. Maybe she wasn't ready to come out to the world. He protected her confidence like he was supposed to do by creating an illusion for the press. I can't believe you would even question that."

"What about the sex?"

"What about it? A guy's gotta have sex, Rachel. *Wake up*."

"You're being a little harsh."

"No I'm not. Look, he probably wasn't attached to any woman at the time they slept together, and she must not have been attached to any man or woman either. Did he ever tell you how long they had known each other?"

"Five years."

"There you go. They had sex before she was involved with this Sherrie person. Maybe what Michael and Tyra had was just for fun. They were just hooking up."

"*Hooking up?*"

"Get with it, Rachel. Hooking up means they were

having casual sex. It's the twenty- first century, girl.'"

"I don't think I like that hooking-up thing. It's morally wrong."

"Look who's talking. You hooked up with Michael at the ski lodge after only knowing him for three or four days."

Rachel stared at her friend.

"Okay, I'm sorry for the way that sounds," Darlene asserted. "But you did. No one is going to question your reasons, Rachel, or judge you. You are a modern woman. You liked the guy, and you trusted him. And it was good therapy for you."

"*Good* for me, Darlene? It just added to my stress!"

"Oh for crying out loud! Your stress was not from that. Your stress was from having your son suddenly diagnosed with a serious disease; from having to rush out of New York to get back to a hospital. You spent weeks at the hospital, and then months afterwards worrying about your little boy. You got backed up in your schoolwork and felt guilty about all the days you took off from work. It probably didn't help that your substitute didn't speak much Spanish and your students complained about her when you came back to school one month later."

"Yeah, I guess so."

"And then you found out about Patrick's secret."

"I know."

"So you've been moping around with all that baggage lately, and God only knows whatever other stressors you've been adding to your suitcase by visiting Dorothy and Paul."

"I know. I know."

They were silent for a few minutes as they ate their

ice-cream.

"Well, did you get your closure when you went to see them?"

"Almost."

"Rachel, you just need to drop it and move on. Please. What else do you want?"

"I want to talk to Jaclyn."

"You're kidding me."

"No, I do. I just want to see what she says."

"You already know what she is going to say! She had an affair. She fell in love with Patrick. And then he broke up with her. Her life fell apart. She moved away. End of story."

"But I need to know why Patrick left me for her. I need to know if I could have done something differently to save our marriage."

"And you think Jaclyn would know the answer to that?"

"No," she sighed. "I guess she didn't give a crap why he strayed; only that he did."

"Things happen for a reason. Even if he had not drifted from your marriage and had not had the affair, you two may not have ended up together. You have to consider that."

"Then what did I do wrong to make him wander off to find someone else? And what did she have that I didn't have?"

"Nothing! Don't you get it? Marriages have their bumps in the road. Some people are strong and they negotiate the hurdles better than others. I'm not saying Patrick was weak. I'm just saying temptation is a very strong obstacle to many marriages. He gave in one day. Maybe if he had been approached by Jaclyn on a different day, he may not have given in. This was not about you. This was about him. It was his problem; don't make it yours."

"How can you say that?"

"You will never know why he did what he did unless you have been approached with the same temptation, Rachel. Stop searching for motives and explanations. Accept that it happened."

"I'll think about it."

"You are one stubborn person, my friend."

"I guess I am," she responded, "but I really do listen to you."

"When are you going?"

"Where?"

"Stop playing. When are you going to see Jaclyn?"

"When school lets out in June. The boys will be going to camp, so I'll go to Maryland where she lives."

"Call her first."

"Why?"

"Because it's the right thing to do."

"Okay."

"Really. Call her."

"Okay, I promise."

"All right. I'm leaving. Gotta go home and make dinner. I know, I had dessert before dinner, but Anthony is waiting for me."

"Okay. Thank you so much, Darlene. Really. You are always there for me."

"I'll always have your back," she answered.

What Rachel didn't know was that Darlene was keeping a secret from her. A big one.

Chapter 21

RACHEL HAD BEEN through plenty of interviews in her lifetime, but none for a winery. How should she prepare for this one? What questions could they possibly ask? She felt like she needed to study and prepare *something*. She read through as much information as she could find on the Internet on the history of wine, about the wineries in Virginia, and about the different types of grapes from the regions nearby. She felt confident about her knowledge of wines, although it couldn't hurt to brush up a bit on the jargon used by the various vintners and reviewers.

Okay, so Thomas Jefferson was a disaster as a winemaker in Virginia, and his exported European vines were trampled by horses, killed by fungus and insects, and destroyed by the cold winters. Virginia's wines were pretty much undrinkable for the next two hundred years, until about forty years ago when they began to taste like something. Not sure what, exactly, because they were certainly unexceptional, but vintners were reconsidering their views about Virginia's soil. Even though the clay soil would get more rain than it could handle, and the high humidity invited the fungus and rotting of grapes, Virginia's winemakers found new ways to mimic the conditions for desirable drainage and air circulation. The Virginia Wine Board Marketing Office reported that there are about two hundred and thirty wineries in the state.

What else should she know? *That's interesting*, she thought, as she read another article. Almost all the wine produced in Virginia is consumed in Virginia, except for about three percent. Could that be true? The article said most of the Virginia wines are consumed at wine festivals and wine tastings. But then the article went on to explain how high-quality winemaking falls out of those statistics. So who are the high-quality winemakers? Is this new winery going to be in that category? Would she be insulting them if she questioned them about it?

Maybe it would be best to stick to the technical stuff. Ask about the slope elevations and altitudes; about pruning practices. Stay on common ground. Talk about the grapes, like the petit verdot, a deep red small grape from loose clusters; or the tannat, a red grape with thick skins. Well, it won't matter what she studies about grapes if those aren't the kinds this winery produces. Or will it? The owner was still experimenting, right? So maybe she could join in on the consideration once she got to know more about their soil conditions and goals for the harvest.

What should she wear?

She decided on a pair of black slacks with a cream-colored button-down shirt, and she'd take a purple jacket with her. Purple would be a good color for a winery, she thought. But it was muggy outside, so she'd wait until the last minute to throw it on before entering the winery. She had picked out some silver earrings that had clusters of grapes on them to compliment the jacket and stick to the theme.

She drove to the winery for her interview, and as she drove up to the entrance, she noticed the sign had been changed to reflect the new name of the establishment: Girasol Winery and Vineyards.

Girasol means Sunflower! My favorite flower! God must be watching over me.

She entered through the familiar doors and walked over to the bar where she saw a tall Mediterranean-looking man standing next to some boxes of what appeared to be tools of some sort. He wore his long dark hair in a ponytail, with a few graying strands escaping and falling onto his shoulders. He was wearing jeans and a long-sleeved white shirt that complimented his tanned and toned body. He could have been the poster guy for a romance novel, she thought.

"Are you Rachel?" he asked coming over to her and extending his hand right away.

"Yes," she responded quickly. "Are you Andreas?"

"I hope so, because *somebody* has to make this wine!"

Good, she thought. A man with a sense of humor.

"So I understand you are interested in a position here for the summer," he said. "Would you continue to work throughout the year on occasional busy weekends or for some of our promotional events?"

"Absolutely! That would be fun."

"Okay, come on over here and we'll get started with some questions, and then I'll show you around."

"I hope you don't mind me asking," Rachel inquired, "but are you the winemaker or the vineyard and operations manager?"

"Jonathan and I split the responsibilities, but we do a lot of the same things. He leads and executes most of the winemaking activities such as crushing, de-stemming, fermentation, aging, and finishing and overseeing the bottling of the wines. He works with the owner in determining, designing and evaluating the wines. I do a lot with the purchasing of equipment, supplies, and labels, and I tabulate the wine inventory. I am also responsible for the marketing initiatives, such as the tastings, dinners and industry events. But I get out in the fields and help with the spring plantings, hedging and tending, and the maintenance of the vineyard when I'm not in the winery behind a spreadsheet. It's beautiful out there, and I have a penchant for watching those little seedlings grow!"

"Wow. You certainly have an exciting job."

"I think so. Anyway, Jon won't be able to meet you today because he and the owner are at another winery discussing some hybrid winemaking philosophies and techniques with a couple of local vintners."

"They don't mind sharing ideas? I mean, aren't the ingredients a secret for their wines?"

"Not really. The soil and location is so diverse, and the care, weather, and amount of ingredients that go into the wines make a big difference in results. Even if two winemakers follow the same recipe in two locations, their wines won't taste the same."

"Oh."

Did that make me sound ignorant?

"But that is all stuff we learn as we go along in this business. Takes years to learn the best practices and combinations. We experiment a lot and we taste a lot of wine."

Whew. I guess every novice is going to be a bit ignorant.

As Rachel and Andreas toured the winery and the grounds, she learned from him that more than eighty percent of the wine produced in Virginia came from grapes grown in the state. He told her the winemaking industry had soared in the past five years and the industry contributed almost three-quarters of a billion dollars to the Commonwealth of Virginia. He also explained most of the industry growth came from small wineries such as theirs, producing approximately ten thousand gallons per year. Only four or five other states had more wineries than Virginia.

"The number of tourists has increased as well," he said, "and as a result, we could use the extra help around here for our events."

"Well I am certainly interested!"

"So what do you know about the wines around here?"

"Well, I know Virginia has about seven major viticulture areas. I know your area specializes in Viognier, Cabernet Franc, and red Bordeaux wines."

"Good. Tell me about the Viognier," he said.

"The Viognier grape is the official grape of Virginia. They believe it possibly came from Croatia. I know it's difficult to grow because it is so prone to mildew, and that means the yield will be unpredictable. It prefers a warmer environment with a longish growing season. I also know it should only be picked when it is fully ripe, not too early, so it doesn't lose its aroma and taste."

"What happens if it is picked too late?" he asked.

"The wine will be oily."

"Perfect. How would you describe it?"

"Floral aromas. Predominantly dry. It needs to be consumed relatively young, like within three years."

"Food pairings?" he probed.

"Spicy foods."

"Excellent. Let's talk about the Cabernet Franc."

She passed the first test. He seemed pleased. She was still a little nervous, but she knew she was answering the questions well.

"The Cab Franc is similar to a Cabernet Sauvignon, but it buds and ripens about one week earlier. It needs a sandy chalk-type soil to produce the heavier wine. It likes cooler areas."

"Taste?" he asked.

"Notes of raspberries, black currants and violets."

"Compared to the Cab Sauvignon?"

"Less tannins than the Sauvignon."

"Finish?" he asked.

"Smooth and balanced. Lingering finish of pepper and nutmeg."

"You know your stuff," he acknowledged. "I'm impressed."

"Can I ask you a question?"

"Shoot away."

"How long do you age your Cab, and what types of barrels do you use?"

"Good question. We age ours around fifteen to sixteen months in oak. We use French, sometimes Hungarian, because the owner doesn't like the spicy addition from the American barrels."

"Also," she continued her questioning, "I noticed some of the vines in the front are not doing so well. What happened?"

"We're letting those go because we're going to use that field for some new hybrids. We'll graph the fruitwood onto some rootstocks we imported from California for a new grape vine plan."

"Rootstock and fruitwood..."

"Don't worry; you won't need to know all of this," he smiled. "But you'll probably pick it up as you hear us talking about it. Rootstock is the lower part of the vine that is responsible for reproduction and fighting off disease. They anchor the plant and take in the nutrients from the soil. The fruitwood is the part of the plant that yields the fruit, so we graph that onto the rootstalk to mold a new wine. We want to be able to design some exclusive hand-crafted wines with special labels for a group of wine investors we've been flirting with."

Rachel laughed. Then she thought maybe her laughter had been inappropriate.

Quick, ask him a question so I don't sound stupid!

"So," she asked, "what types of wine drinkers do you feel this winery will attract?"

"Well, we know there are a lot of new wine drinkers these days. The younger crowds are starting to catch on to the winery weekends and are straying a bit from the breweries. So we know we have to attract the new drinkers with a sweeter wine. We're looking at the Norton grape for that. It's very popular here in Virginia. But we are also targeting the more experienced connoisseurs, so we're perfecting our Cab and Viognier, and we're introducing a new Chardonnay."

"What is your strategy?" she asked.

"People to the bottle. The owner is quite wealthy and not so interested in delivering wines to the retail and restaurant marketplace. He is more interested in bringing people to the winery to tour the place, taste the wines, and then purchase bottles from the winery."

"I love it. It has a warm personal feeling about it," she said waving her arm around.

"It does. So, do you have any more questions for me?" he asked.

"Oh, I'm so sorry! You are supposed to be asking me all the questions!"

"I'm just kidding, Rachel." After a few moments, "I think you are a good fit for this winery. I'd like to offer you the job."

"I'll take it!" she blurted out and then turned beet red.

"I love your enthusiasm. We need people like you to join our family."

"So when would I start?"

"Let's get started the first week of July. We just got the place in February, so we are waiting for the mandated six-month licenses, but we expect to open in mid-July with a big bash. I'd like to have you here full-time for a couple of weeks before the opening."

RACHEL DROVE HOME from the winery feeling elated for the first time since Lake Placid. She counted her blessings: Andrew was well and had been given clean check-ups by his team of doctors; Brandon was happy and still had his little girlfriend from school; she had friends, a nice home, a car that was paid off, and now this fantastic job. What else could she possibly want?

It would have been nice to have had a significant other to share these moments with; someone who would have been excited for her and would have been proud of her interview at the winery. But that would come.

No more online dating, though. Not that she had even looked at the site since she had returned from Lake Placid, but that part of her life was over. It was too stressful. Hopefully her prince charming would walk through the doors of the winery someday. If not, screw it. There was much more to life than spending time worrying about meeting a man.

Chapter 22

RACHEL SHIFTED BACK and forth on her feet as she gazed at the number on the door inside the lavish Bethesda apartment complex. Finally she summoned enough courage to knock. Her resolve had been a lot stronger earlier in the day on her road trip to Maryland than it was at this moment.

"Hello, Jaclyn," she said, as the other woman opened the door.

"Hi, Rachel," the woman responded in a barely audible voice.

Rachel had called ahead of time to ask if Jaclyn would be receptive to her visit. Not that it would eliminate Jaclyn's uneasiness when facing the woman whose husband she had stolen, but Rachel had known calling in advance had been the noble thing to do, as Darlene had said.

"Please, come on in," she motioned reluctantly to Rachel as she stepped aside to let her in.

"Thanks, but I don't want to intrude; I'll just stay out here."

"Okay." Jaclyn responded awkwardly, having no idea what to anticipate from the woman standing across the threshold.

Rachel could not have known Jaclyn had wanted to beg her forgiveness and explain how she had fallen in love with her husband but had never intended to hurt her. *It happens*, she had wanted to say. Men can't just wear signs saying *taken* and then expect women to not be attracted to them. Souls find each other, no matter how hard one fights the urge to act on the discovery. But she had acted on it, hadn't she?

"Rachel, I'm so—"

"No, it's okay," she responded holding up her hand.

Here it goes.

Rachel had thought for weeks about what she would say to this woman if she had had the opportunity. She had written notes and had rehearsed speeches over and over again in her mind. Each time the speech was different. Today it would be different.

"I'm sorry too," Rachel finally said.

"What?" Jaclyn asked softly as she searched Rachel's face for an indication she had heard her incorrectly.

"I know you loved him too," Rachel continued, "and he hurt us both. I think he was hurting too."

The silence pierced the air as the women stood in the doorway.

"He chose you, you know," the woman finally said to Rachel.

"So I was told. I visited Dorothy. And Paul."

"Yes, he told me."

Rachel had been looking down at the floor in the hallway, and Jaclyn had been playing with the door handle to steady her nerves as she listened to Patrick's wife.

"Okay. I have to leave now," Rachel said at last.

"Rachel—"

"It's okay."

Rachel rummaged in the heavy bag balanced on her shoulder, found what she was looking for, and handed it to Jaclyn. She turned and slowly walked away towards the elevators at the end of the hall, and she never looked back.

Jaclyn looked down at the bundle of letters in her hand; letters she had written to Patrick that last year of his life. She hadn't known he had kept them, until today. She wished she had kept the letters he had written to her, but she had been too afraid her husband would find them. Now she had nothing left of Patrick.

And yet, she had known he was never hers to begin with.

Jaclyn gently closed the door.

Chapter 23

RACHEL DROVE THE thirty minutes from Bethesda to Arlington National Cemetery as a heavy rain pounded on her windshield. She passed through the imposing gates of the cemetery and drove directly to the place where Patrick was inurned.

She stood in front of the cold square block of marble behind which her husband lay in peace. It was dark and damp in the columbarium. Even so, she felt a sense of warmth come over her, as if Patrick's spirit was enveloping her. There had been much written about spirits lingering on earth until they could consummate their unfinished business.

"Patrick," she whispered tenderly as she touched his name engraved on the stone wall in front of her, "If you are here, I'd like you to listen to this letter."

She took the letter from her pocket, unfolded it, and began slowly reading the words she had scripted the night before.

My dearest Patrick,
Thank you for our beautiful children. I will never re-

gret choosing you as the father of our boys. You were a good father, and they have grown into the young men I know you would have been proud of. I promise to take care of them and keep them safe for as long as I live.

I found the key to your safe deposit box. You probably already know.

I was angry at you for a long time. All my wonderful memories were turned into ugly ones as I reconsidered the pictures of our years together. I wondered if there had been other women, not just Jaclyn. I hated you for what you did to our family. I broke your picture in the hallway and threw you away from my heart. Then I thought maybe I had been the reason for your infidelity, and I felt guilty and unworthy of anyone's attention, much less their love. I pushed people away. I was so sad; I thought I would never recover from the hurt.

There were and are so many unanswered questions. But I'm going to file them away in a folder in the back of my heart, because I know I will never have your answers; only my assumptions. I've come to terms with that.

It must have been awful keeping your secret about Jaclyn. I can only assume you were as conflicted about our love as you were about wanting her. I'm sorry if I ever hurt you, or if I ever pushed you away. I hope you knew in the end how much I loved you, Patrick. I think you were sorry you hurt me too. I know you loved me; I felt it the night before you left for Bahrain.

Thank you for not telling other people about your affair with Jaclyn and for protecting me and the children from what could have been.

I've learned secrets don't remain hidden forever, and

they condemn people to living in fear of their discovery. I'm so sorry you had to live that way. I have to admit I hate the responsibility that goes with owning your secret. I've had the added burden of deciding whether or not to tell the boys, your parents, and your friends. But you can trust me, I never will. There is no point in hurting anyone else.

I don't want to destroy Brandon and Andrew's image of you. They look up to you so much. You are their hero. You should have heard Brandon's speech about you at school when they had to do a presentation on the person they most admire. He wants to follow in your footsteps, you know, and join the military. I guess I still have a few years to get used to the idea! I'm not sure what Andrew wants to do yet. I'm just glad he's alive and well. Were you there, Patrick? In the hospital room with him? He talked about you a lot, so I wondered... They miss you. So does Oliver. I still catch him going into your closet every now and then and smelling your clothes or shoes. He lays in there all bundled up when there is a thunderstorm. Maybe you're still taking care of him too.

You were a respectable man, Patrick. The affair didn't define you. You were a good father, a decent provider, a hard worker, and a worthy friend. Sometimes we just lose our way. Sometimes marriage changes into a comfortable relationship or partnership that is still meaningful, and still fulfilling. We had that, didn't we? If you had truly loved Jaclyn, I would not have stood in your way. I know that now, and I wanted you to know it too. We can't control others' feelings.

It's time for me to say good-bye. I feel stronger now, and I'm ready to move on. I don't know what changed.

Maybe it was a combination of factors: the passing of time, the help from friends, or the prospect of my summer job at the winery. And there are the boys, or course. The thought of losing Andrew has made me realize life is precious, every single moment of it. I don't want to live in the shadow of love misunderstood; I want to welcome a new love, whenever that happens in this journey. I know you would have wanted that for me.

Good-bye, my love.

She delicately folded the paper and tucked it away in her purse. She'd have to remember to throw it away before going home so it could never be found. It was private.

Rachel took out of her pocket the brass heart key Patrick had given her, the one she had worn around her neck so often. She had strung it on a red ribbon. She ran her fingers along the silk filament gazing nostalgically at the trinket for a long moment, as if she was parting with an old friend.

She glanced around the columbarium looking for a spot where she could leave the key. She saw a sparkle in the dim light of the room on the floor directly in front of her, something she hadn't noticed before, and she bent down to see what was generating the disorder in this solemn place of rest.

It was the second key, the identical twin.

She knew instinctively it had been placed there by her husband's other love.

She picked it up, laced the red ribbon through both keys, and then gently placed them on the floor in front of her husband's dwelling.

"Rest in peace, Patrick."

RACHEL TOOK OUT her cell phone and texted Darlene as she sat in her car at the Cemetery.

I'm ready, she texted.

For what? Darlene replied.

For anything, she responded.

Chapter 24

"HELLO?" DARLENE CLUMSILY answered her cell phone while shifting packages into her other hand on the doorstep.

"Hi, Darlene," came the voice from the other end.

"Hey," she answered abruptly, "give me a second to open my door, okay? I'm just getting back from a shopping spree."

"I can call back if this is a bad time."

"No, actually it's a good time. Just one sec."

Darlene unlocked the newly painted door to the house she and Anthony had purchased in early June. She was spending the summer getting it ready for their move at the end of July. Painting and re-carpeting the house, mending the gutters, and cleaning up the jungle in their garden was certainly an overzealous goal while planning a wedding at the same time. They had found this wonderful fixer-upper and had fallen in love with it on the spot. They had submitted their bid the same day they saw the house, and then the negotiating began against another prospective client in a minor war-of-the-brides. The other bride never had a chance against Darlene.

"Sorry to keep you," she said, throwing her packages of matching towels and linens on the floor inside the door. "How are you, Michael?"

"Good! How are the projects going on your new house?"

"Oh God," she sighed, "some days we make a lot of progress, and other days we just muddle along pretending we know what we are doing. Neither one of us is a carpenter or a plumber, so we're just doing our best!"

"I hear you! I'm learning those skills too right now. Darned if I know how to fix this roof. And I'm getting annoyed with all this rain," he commiserated.

"Hey, no pain no gain, right?"

"True. So how is Rachel, Darlene?"

"She's doing okay, Mike. She's really excited about her new part-time job at the winery for the summer. And she's looking forward to going to the beach for a week in August."

"And the boys?" he asked.

"They just came back from a camp at the lake, and this week their grandparents took them for a vacation to Arizona. Next month they'll go to their daytime baseball camp, and then to the beach with Rachel. Those boys have more energy than I ever had, that's for sure!"

"Andrew's still getting good check-ups?"

"Absolutely. He's cured, for all intent and purpose."

"That is truly good news. I really appreciate you keeping me informed, Darlene. I know this is difficult for you, not telling Rachel we have been in touch."

"Thanks for understanding, Mike," she sighed. "I do feel awkward about this whole clandestine thing, you know?"

"I know," he said delicately. "And I appreciate it."

"I just don't want Rachel to think I'm a traitor, you know? I mean, she *hates* secrets, and I don't want to lose her friendship."

"I don't want to put you in an uncomfortable position, either. We can stop if you want."

"No, I know this is right." She stalled for a moment as if to reassure herself. "I know Rachel will understand once we finish this covert operation."

Michael smiled at the image *covert operation* conjured in his mind: two spies draped in raincoats and sunglasses trying to conceal their identities as they surreptitiously followed their suspect. Only Rachel was not a suspect. She was the woman he adored. He wondered if she would think he had been stalking her through her friend once she found out about them. He wasn't even sure if Rachel would feel the same as he felt for her, but he had to trust his instincts. He had promised her at Lake Placid six months ago that if she were ever lost, he would find her. And he had found her. She just didn't know it yet.

"Listen, I have a few things to tie up here in California, but I'll be back east in a couple of weeks," he said. "Do you think Rachel would be willing to see me then?"

"We're going to try, Michael, we're going to try," she responded.

MICHAEL AND DARLENE had been exchanging phone calls since late January, ever since he had been told by Erin that Darlene was Rachel's friend and confidant.

Michael had had no idea how to find Rachel in Virginia after she had abruptly left the lodge at Lake Placid. They hadn't exchanged contact information, and he hadn't even known what town she lived in or where she worked. Then he had remembered Rachel had used Erin's phone at the village to call him the night they went tobogganing with the boys. Sure enough, he had been able to scroll back in his received calls and had been able to identify Erin's phone number.

He had been devastated by how the scene at the resort had ended. Rachel had misunderstood what she had seen. But Michael had known he had needed to give her some space, so he had left her alone.

Several weeks into January, Michael had decided enough time had lapsed, and he had boldly called Erin to request Rachel's phone number. Erin had told him it would not be wise to call Rachel at that time, explaining she was overwhelmed by her life events. Michael had spent time explaining to Erin the best he could what he felt Rachel had misconstrued between him and Tyra. Erin had asked for his respectful distance and some time while Andrew recovered from surgery, but she had concluded their exchange by giving him Darlene's number as the next step to making contact. Erin had later called Darlene and had given her the heads-up.

Darlene had felt guilty about the prospect of talking to Michael on the phone, but she had gone with her gut and had agreed to talk to him. She would give him the basics about how Rachel was doing, but she would never surrender her friend's trust. Ultimately Darlene had felt Rachel would need to confront her feelings for Michael, whether it ended well for him or not.

When Darlene had received her first phone call from Michael, they had spent some time getting acquainted. She had felt uncomfortable asking him about what had happened at the ski lodge in December, but he had volunteered as much information as he could. He had not wanted to break Tyra's trust in him, so he had told Darlene the matter would become clearer later on. Darlene had respected his explanation, and she had accepted his request to keep in touch.

She could tell Michael loved Rachel and he was not going to give up the fight whether she had agreed to help him or not. She admired him. This was exactly what her friend had needed, she concluded, a man who loved her fully and unconditionally; someone who was willing to pursue her to the ends of the earth. You can't turn off true love, Darlene had thought. She remembered what Shakespeare had once said, *the course of true love never did run smooth.* And this was certainly not a smooth path they would have to travel. But she was sure Michael's love for Rachel was genuine love worth having. It may still be hiding under all the debris on the road, Darlene believed, but it was there just the same. She would have to help Rachel and Michael find it by picking up the fallen branches in their way.

What Darlene and Michael hadn't expected to get in the way of their plan, however, was the revelation that came after Andrew's ordeal in the hospital: Patrick's deceitful infidelity. Darlene believed an encounter between them at that point could be damaging. Michael had understood. He would wait.

Michael had told Darlene he could relate to the main character of Gabriel García Márques' book: *Love in the Time of Cholera*. The protagonist, Florentino Ariza, had fallen passionately in love with Fermina Díaz. But Fermina had chosen to marry a wealthy doctor instead, leaving Florentino to a life of unrequited love. Fifty years later, Fermina's husband died, and Florentino found himself going to the funeral to declare his everlasting love to her.

Yes, Michael could wait. He had the rest of his life to wait.

SEVERAL MONTHS AFTER the initial contact between Darlene and Michael, the tabloids published the news of Tyra Milano's engagement to her partner Sherrie. Michael had promised clarity, and there it was. He had not broken his promise to Tyra in revealing her romance with her partner until it had hit the news.

Michael had explained to Darlene that he and Ms. Milano had met when she was a young aspiring actress. Her agent had come to Michael when he had been exploring the film production business as an investment, and the agent had beseeched him to take a look at her work. Michael had spoken to the director of the indie film for which she had auditioned, and the director had confirmed the star had talent that assured her a promising future. Michael had agreed to support her and produce her first movie. The venture paid off handsomely, and Michael had decided to continue investing in film production. Tyra had become an instantaneous celebrity and Michael's friend.

Early in their friendship, Michael and Tyra had slept together for one night after weeks of grueling work prior to the film's release. Michael had been trying to keep his law practice fluid, and at the same time juggle the demands of film production. Tyra had been overworked with publicity engagements and trips to promote the film in the States and overseas. They had fallen into bed one night after a few glasses of wine. It had meant nothing; just an act to relieve stress. It hadn't changed anything between them. Tyra had eventually fallen in love with Sherrie, and Michael had become involved in a long-termed relationship himself. Around the time his own relationship had fallen apart, the media had begun questioning Tyra's affiliation with Sherrie. In order to save her career, her team had decided she needed to either come clear about her romance with Sherrie, or find a man who would cover for her. Tyra had not been ready to explain her orientation to her parents. Michael had stepped in and had volunteered to be her cover. No one had questioned their romance; only they had known it was fabricated.

He had never truly fallen in love, or at least not enough to spend the rest of his life with someone. That is, until he had met Rachel. Well, until he had met her *again*. He had thought about her constantly after their time in New York. *I'm going to marry that lady*, he had told his friend Ian when he had seen Rachel at the ski shop that December day.

After the fallout at the lodge, however, Michael had returned to California. He had begun running and working long hours to get his mind off Rachel. But he couldn't. So he began making his decisions, small and large, with her in mind. Rachel had not known about Michael's intentions, but he had decided to do everything possible to pave the way for the possibility of their future together. He withdrew from the movie business and named an associate as senior partner of his law firm, just in case he would have to move to Virginia. He had never made such sacrifices for a woman. He had been married to his job for his entire adult life. He had focused on winning cases in court, funding new projects, pursuing thrilling exploits in foreign countries, and investing in high-risk ventures; but he had never imagined giving it all up for a woman.

He had decided to tell his daughter Ellie about Rachel. It's funny how children respond to things one has hesitated telling them for fear of alienating them or making them jealous. Ellie had been attached to her father's hip from the day he had brought her home to California when she had been three years old. Dad and daughter had had to learn how to become an instant family. They had learned through trial and error, but they had come out on top. They had fostered a bond that was impenetrable. He had not wanted Ellie to feel their relationship was being threatened by Rachel, so he had wanted to wait to talk to her until the time felt right. Well, there never *is* a right time, he had decided.

Ellie had listened intently without saying a word when Michael had told her about Rachel.

"Do you have any questions?" he had asked her.

"Will I have any brothers or sisters?" she had responded.

And that was that.

Michael was ready to declare his love to Rachel as

soon as she was emotionally available.

Darlene had just assured him on the phone it was time.

Chapter 25

IT WAS THE middle of July and Darlene had been invited to the soft opening of the Girasol Winery where Rachel and her associates would be pouring wine to a select group of patrons. The winery would open to the public the following week if everything went well with the trial.

Coincidentally, Darlene had ordered labels for the bottles of wine that would be served at her wedding, and Elizabeth had called to let her know the samples were ready. Perfect timing.

Darlene drove along the winding road festooned with throngs of white delicate daisies until she saw the sign for the newly refurbished winery. She turned and drove up the path lined by sunflowers and parked her car in the lot adjacent to the estate. She recognized Rachel's car in the lot, and she drew a few nervous breaths as she rehearsed how she would approach the subject of Michael with her friend. Today was the day.

When she opened the doors to the French chateau, she was lured inside by the aromas of the new wines that had been crafted specifically for this inaugural day. The fragrances rose to the vaulted ceilings above counters where bottles sat opened and waiting. There were tall bright yellow sunflowers in colorful ceramic vases scattered throughout the main room. A trio of jazz musicians was assembled in one corner playing smooth tunes to accompany the perfumes of the wine dancing in midair.

Darlene approached the counter where she saw Elizabeth talking to a few customers while pouring a luscious dark red Chambourcin.

"What I'd like you to do," she was saying, "is to take a taste of this. Swirl it around in your mouth and remember your perception. Now take a bite of this brownie." She waited a moment. "Now taste the wine again." Another moment. "Does it change?"

"Yes!" one woman responded.

"How so?" Elizabeth probed.

"It was a bit jammy up front. But now it's pleasant, and a bit drier," the lady responded as she twirled the wine in her glass and took another sip.

"Good. Anyone else?"

"It doesn't have the unpleasant hybrid flavors that some Chambourcins have," one man responded.

Must be a wine snob, Darlene thought, *who isn't a big fan of hybrids.*

But Elizabeth was obviously ready for the comments that came her way. She handled the client with his due respect. After all, wine preferences are different for everyone, so not being an aficionado for some varietals is perfectly natural.

"That is a good observation," Elizabeth responded. "You have a trained nose. The hybrid grape was produced in the 1860's in France, but it has only been available to us here since around 1963, and we are happy for the discovery. Our Chambourcin tends to be a little bit dry, the way we prefer it here at Girasol, instead of one with a moderate residual sugar level with a sweeter taste."

Darlene observed another man nodding and agreeing with her delivery.

"What do you ferment it in?" asked a customer.

"We use French oak. Our Chambourcin has low acidity and soft tannins, but it can carry itself well in French barrels. Any other questions?"

No one responded.

"Okay, then I'm going to have you move into the other room with Rachel to talk about the Viognier. Later Andreas will be taking you on a tour of the cellars, and Jonathan will take you through the vineyard."

The group followed Elizabeth through the archway to the next room and Darlene caught a glimpse of Rachel coming over to greet them. She decided to stay away from her friend so she wouldn't feel nervous about her presentation with her first group of guests. Instead, she approached Elizabeth.

"Oh, Darlene, I'm glad you were able to make it today! I am so excited about showing you the wine bottle labels I designed for your wedding!"

Elizabeth was planning to study graphic design at the Moore College of Art in Philadelphia in the fall, and Darlene could already tell she would be a great success in her chosen field.

"Well, let's take a look."

"Okay, I've got them in a binder over here."

She pulled the binder from one of the shelves and put

it on the counter.

"Do you mind if I try that Chambourcin you were talking about while we look at your designs?" Darlene asked.

"Of course!" Elizabeth poured her a glass.

"I enjoyed your talk."

"Ah, nothing to it!"

"Wow," Darlene exclaimed as she opened the binder and pulled out the designs. "I am loving these labels, lady!"

Elizabeth's smile couldn't have been any wider.

"Okay, I think I like this one for the Chardonnay, this one for the red wine, and this one for the sparkling wine. But I only need three labels and I like this one over here too. Agh! Do you have a favorite?"

Elizabeth turned the binder to face her way and looked at the six labels she had designed. Just then Darlene got a text message from Michael.

Is today still the day?

Yes, she texted back. *I'll call you.*

At that moment Rachel walked into the room. "Hey, look at those beautiful wine labels!" she said as she approached the bar.

"I know, right? Which ones would you choose, Rach? I can only choose three."

"Oh no you don't! I'm not going to hear Anthony say I chose for him! You need to take them home and let *him* choose!" Turning to Elizabeth, "That really is nice work. You are so artistic."

"Gracias!"

"Hey," Rachel said turning to Darlene, "do you want to join Andreas' tour in the wine cellar since you're already here? He really does a nice job explaining the process of wine-making."

"Sure. But I want to talk to you about something along the way."

"Okay."

They walked down a steep iron staircase to the passages underground where the wine slept until it was ready for its reveal. Andreas' voice echoed from a dark chamber nearby as he explained his craft to the visitors. Darlene gasped at the sight in front of her as she and her friend rounded the corner to join the guests. There were endless rows of oak barrels barely visible in the golden aura emitted by candles surrounding Andreas and the guests. He was speaking to them in hushed tones as he dipped into a barrel with a long glass tube.

"We missed his speech about the history of this winery, but I can fill you in on that later," Rachel whispered to her friend.

Okay," she whispered back. "What is that glass thing he's putting in the barrel?"

"It's a *wine thief*," Rachel answered with a little giggle.

"A what?"

"They dip it into the barrels and hold their finger on the other side so it collects wine to taste. Kind of like a turkey baster."

"But the wine looks cloudy that he pulled out."

"It is. It hasn't been finished yet, you know, filtered, but it's exceptionally drinkable," Rachel clarified.

"Oh. I guess I sound stupid."

"Not at all! I had to learn this myself. I'm just showing off for you," she said laughing quietly. "Do you want to taste some of it?"

"Actually, I wanted to talk to you for a few minutes."

"What is it?" Rachel asked as she looked into her friend's troubled face. "Are you and Anthony okay?"

"Yes, of course. But I wanted to ask you the same."

"What do you mean?"

"Are *you* okay, Rachel?"

"I haven't been this happy in a long time, Darlene."

"Okay," she took a deep breath, "then I think you should call Michael Blanford."

There, she said it. She hoped Rachel wouldn't scream and wake up all the grapes in the cellar.

"Darlene, I'm not sure if I'm following you."

"Then hear me out. When you called me from Lake Placid back in December, you were head over heels crazy about Michael. You said you had never dreamed about getting a second chance at love. Even Erin told me she saw the sparks between you two."

"Erin?"

"Wait, keep listening," Darlene said putting her hand on Rachel's arm.

"You fell in love. But you saw something in the lobby between Michael and Tyra Milano that you misinterpreted, so you ran away from love."

"I didn't—"

"Yes you did, Rach. You misconstrued what you saw, and you bolted. I showed you that magazine. Tyra is, *was*, not with Michael. And I don't care what you say about the sex thing. They had sex once; more power to them. You had sex with Michael once too, so I don't see how that is any different."

"But—"

"No, Rach. It isn't any different. In any case, you rushed off to take care of Andrew after what you had seen in the lobby, and you were determined to believe Michael didn't love you."

"What do you mean?"

"I mean you felt guilty you weren't with Andrew when he fell. You thought you had neglected your children and didn't deserve to be happy, so you took your anger out on Michael and Tyra. It's easier to run away than to have to face conflict."

"I didn't run away."

"Yes you did. Who is the counselor here, Rach?"

They were both quiet for a moment.

"Anyway, then you went through the two-month ordeal with Andrew back at the hospital. After all of that stress, you resumed your little life in your cocoon of a home with all your little routines so everything would become safe again."

"No, that's not true."

"Yes it is. You know it is. You pushed Michael out of your mind and out of your heart. You let that heart of yours become as hard as a rock, and you put up a plexiglas exterior that no one could permeate. Michael had managed to get in when your guard was down, but you were determined to not let it happen again."

"Is that what I did?" she asked sincerely.

"Yes. And it doesn't have to be that way. If you never let anyone in, your house is going to be empty for the rest of your life. Then you'll look around at the lonely chambers of your heart, and you'll wish you had at least tried for the right person. After Michael, I'm betting no one else will measure up to him, and then you'll never let anyone in. Am I right?"

"I guess so. I'm just afraid I'll uncover another secret like Patrick's, and the next time it happens, I won't have the strength to deal with it."

Darlene knew this was going to be the hard part of her intervention.

"I have a secret I've been keeping from you, Rachel."

There it is.

"What?" she responded barely audible with disbelief slowly registering on her features.

"I have been talking to Michael."

"You *what*?"

"Michael and I have been talking about you since January. He got my number from Erin and called to ask how you and the boys have been doing. He loves you, Rach."

"*Erin*? You and Erin kept this a secret from me?"

Rachel turned and walked towards the stairs. She climbed them quickly and went straight for the door to the outside. She was gasping for air as her eyes filled with tears.

"Rachel!"

Rachel turned and looked at her friend with incredulity.

Darlene had prepared for this; she knew what to say.

"Stop, Rachel. You are overreacting."

"You think I'm overreacting to one of my best friends keeping a secret from me? Am I going to find out you knew about Patrick too?"

"No. I didn't know about Patrick. And this here, this I just shared with you, it isn't a secret."

"Then you tell me what it is, Darlene. Because in my book, friends don't keep important information like this from each other. They share. I guess this is what I get for telling anyone about Michael in the first place."

"Rachel, I don't deserve that, and you know it. But I'm going to let it slide because I know you're upset and it's more comfortable to be stubborn than to have to deal with conflict."

Rachel walked slowly down the gravel road away from the winery as tangled thoughts flooded into her head. She knew she had been too abrupt in her comments to her friend. Darlene was right; she hated conflict. She knew she was a runner. This hadn't been the first time she had run away from her stressors. She did fall in love with Michael. She did bolt, as Darlene had said. Maybe it had been because she was afraid of moving out to California, leaving her job and her friends, wondering if the boys would adjust to a new environment. Maybe she did use the scene at the lobby as an excuse to avoid facing those issues.

"Okay, so let's talk about secrets," Darlene interrupted her friend's thoughts.

"I know, I'm sorry. I shouldn't have made those comments to you. But you know I *hate* secrets."

"Look, a secret is something that is concealed or hidden from others, right? But that doesn't mean the intent is always deceitful. I could have planned a secret birthday party for you. Someone could have bought you a secret gift. Or maybe you aren't telling me your secret ingredient to that spaghetti sauce of yours because you think I'll make mine better than yours!"

Rachel smiled through her tears.

"Don't get caught up on the word, Rachel. Having a secret does not mean someone is harboring something unethical or devious, okay? It can be good too."

"Why did you keep it from me? I mean, I get it, but why?"

"I was protecting you, my dear friend. You weren't ready. Michael knew you weren't ready."

"He did?"

"Yes."

"And now?"

"We think you are ready."

Rachel hugged her friend. "Okay, I think I get it."

"So will you call him for me?"

"Right now?" she asked wiping away her tears with the sleeve of her shirt.

"Only if you want."

"Can we walk for a little bit first until I get up my nerve?"

"Of course. But don't take too long, because I'm missing the wine presentation inside."

Chapter 26

RACHEL AND DARLENE reentered the winery and chose a cozy little table near the bar where they could make the private call to Michael. Both groups of invited guests had filtered out to the vineyards to listen to Jonathan's talk about how he had designed the wine they drank earlier. The winery was not expecting another group for half an hour, so Rachel knew she had time to make the call Darlene had wanted her to make.

"Are you sure I should do this?"

"You are a crazy lady, you know that?" Darlene responded shaking her head back and forth.

"Okay, give me the number."

"Shoot, I left my cell phone in the car with the number."

"Darlene!"

"I'm just messing with you. Here. Add this contact to your cell phone so you don't have to bother me again."

Rachel was laughing at her friend. Darlene had a way of calming her down; of helping her see the other side of everything.

"Here goes." Rachel punched in the number, took a big

breath, and grabbed Darlene's arm.

"Hello?"

"Hi. Is this Mike?"

"Rachel?"

"Yes. Um, Darlene told me that you wanted me to call you."

What a stupid thing to say!

"I did! I'm so glad you called, Rachel. I miss you."

"You do?"

Another stupid thing to say!

"Yes," he laughed.

"Thanks. I guess I missed you too."

Darlene gave her a look.

"I mean, I miss you too," she corrected herself while looking at her friend. She mouthed to her *now what do I say?*

"Rachel, I'd love to see you and try to explain everything."

"I'd like that."

"Where are you?" he asked.

"I'm here. I mean, I'm at a winery in Virginia. I'm working here for the summer. So that's where I am right now." She knew she was stumbling over her words.

"Are you on a break? I don't want to get you into trouble with the boss by talking on the phone."

"Yes, I'm on a break. We're between groups. Today is a VIP day and we only have four groups of people coming through. We open officially next week after we get all their feedback today."

"You said you always wanted to work in a winery. I'm so glad you have the opportunity to do so."

"Me too. It's fun."

"I wish I could see you right now," he said, hoping she would feel the same.

"Me too."

"Then turn around," he said.

"What?" she asked while looking at Darlene and pointing to her phone with a confused frown on her face.

Darlene motioned for her to turn around in her chair.

Rachel dropped her phone. Michael was standing by the bar with his phone to his ear.

She looked back and forth from Michael to her friend as her mind struggled to register what her eyes were seeing.

"Can I get you a glass of wine?" he asked as he approached her with a bottle of Chambourcin and a big smile on his face. He was as nervous as she, but he had hoped his casual approach would dispel any possible apprehension at seeing him so unexpectedly.

Rachel was speechless.

"I don't think the boss would mind," he said, as he poured the wine into a couple of glasses he had brought with him.

"Michael, I haven't even met the boss, and I don't want the winemaker to think I'm breaking the rules. We really shouldn't…"

Her sentence was interrupted when he pulled her out of the chair and kissed her passionately on the lips.

She pulled slightly away and looked into his face for reassurance. Then she threw her arms around him and kissed him with every ounce of emotion that had been dormant since their last encounter.

"Hi, dad!" Elizabeth said entering the room.

"Hi, pumpkin," Michael responded as Rachel nervously pushed him away.

"Elizabeth is your *daughter*?" she asked incredulous.

"Yes. This is my Ellie."

"Dad, I'm *Elizabeth*, not Ellie," she corrected him.

"Okay, okay. *Elizabeth* is trying out her birth name before going to college. She thinks 'Ellie' isn't grown-up enough."

"Elizabeth is *Ellie*?"

"Mary Elizabeth Blanford. The one and only," Michael responded with a proud smile.

"Like your aunt Mary Katherine?" Rachel asked Ellie as she turned to face her.

"And my mom, Mary Grace. So how do you two know each other?" Ellie pointed back and forth between Michael and Rachel.

"This is the Rachel I spoke to you about, Ellie."

"This is *that* Rachel? The one you met at Lake Placid?!"

"Yes," he responded with a smile.

"Rachel!" Ellie ran up to her and hugged her, "I didn't know it was *you*! My dad *loves* you! I didn't know you were the same Rachel he loves! I'm so happy!"

Rachel was smiling and hugging Ellie as she looked at Michael.

"I had no idea you were Ellie," she said. "Can I call you *Ellie*?"

"Yes!"

"Hey, she can call you Ellie but I have to call you Elizabeth?" Michael asked feigning offense.

Rachel turned to Darlene, "Did you know this was

Mike's daughter?"

"No."

Rachel looked at her a bit suspect.

"Really, Rach, I didn't know. I just knew Michael owned this winery, but I didn't put two-and-two together to figure Elizabeth was his daughter."

"*You own the winery?*" Rachel turned towards Michael.

"I do."

"Okay, then give me that glass. I need a drink!" she responded.

They all laughed and Michael went to the bar for a couple more glasses.

"When did you buy it?" she asked him when he returned.

"I bought it in February after talking to Darlene and finding out what you wanted to do this summer. The Lotus Winery just happened to be for sale, and I was at the right place at the right time."

"You bought a winery because Darlene told you I wanted to work at one over the summer? You took a big chance!"

"I did," he responded pulling her back into his arms, "and you are worth it. I don't know if you remember me telling you in December that I was seriously looking into buying a winery out in California. But after our chance meeting at the lodge, I decided California was too far away."

Rachel smiled and looked around the room. "Why haven't I ever seen you here?"

"I've been travelling between the west coast and here.

I had to wrap things up at the law firm in California."

"You quit your firm?"

"Kind of. I left it with a couple of partners. I'll need to go out there probably once every quarter. Maybe a little more to begin with."

"What about the movie business?"

"Done with that." He cocked his head, "Did Darlene explain about my friend Tyra?"

"Oh, Tyra," Ellie interjected. "She is so cool, isn't she?"

"You know her?" Rachel asked.

"Yeah, she took care of me. I mean, *we hung out*, when dad was on his business trips."

"Yeah, you're too old to be taken care of, right?" her dad laughed and grabbed her head in an elbow-lock to plant a kiss on her hair.

"Rachel, I didn't see you at Lake Placid," Ellie said ignoring her playful father.

"You were there?"

"Yeah. I went with Tyra. When dad told me he was staying a few more days, we flew out to surprise him. But I guess you were gone."

"Yes," Rachel fidgeted. "My son Andrew had a fall on the ski slope."

"Is he okay now? So when do I get to see my new broth…" she caught herself and put her hand to her mouth and then looked at her dad apologetically.

"Didn't I tell you Ellie was 17 going on 30?" Michael said rolling his eyes.

"*Eighteen last week*, dad!"

Rachel laughed. "Yes, Andrew is okay. Thanks for

asking."

"You saw Ellie in the lobby the day you left," Michael told her.

"I thought that was Tyra's daughter! That was *you* in the fur coat and high boots?"

"Yeah! Tyra and I like to match our outfits. She's so cool. Everyone thinks she's my mom because I'm light brown like her."

Ellie was obviously a light-skinned African American, but Rachel was too embarrassed to ask for clarification.

"My grandfather was black, and my grandma was white. I've never met them. They kind of disowned me," Ellie said matter-of-factly. "But I'm cool with that. My mom loved me, and my Aunt Mary Katherine loves me. Anyway, that's why I'm this color. You know, because my mom was a mixture of black and white. Neat, huh?"

"Yes, it is. You are a *gorgeous* color, Ellie."

She was falling in love with Ellie. This girl, or *young lady*, was very down-to-earth. She called things the way she saw them. She was mature beyond her years, probably because she had grown up with a single father. Maybe because she was around movie stars and lawyers all the time.

Michael's quick explanation had cleared up her confusion about what she had seen in the lobby at the ski lodge back in December. Ellie had come to surprise her dad, and Tyra had come along as her guardian.

I owe Tyra a big apology! I'm such an idiot. And Michael was only trying to protect her secret. Secrets—ugh! What had Darlene said earlier? That secrets aren't always deceitful? Tyra's secret certainly wasn't deceitful; she had just not been ready to expose her personal life to the public eye, and it wasn't anyone else's business anyway.

"Michael," Rachel said, "I'm so sorry for the way I acted."

"Shh," he said hugging her tightly.

"Okay," Darlene sang to Ellie, "so how about you take me on a tour of the vineyards and we join Jonathan and Andreas out there. I need to learn about some grapes!"

The two of them giggled, joined arms, and walked out the door.

"Michael, did I get this job at the winery because you are the owner?"

"No," he said honestly looking down into her eyes. "Scouts honor." He put up three fingers.

"It's such a weird coincidence!"

"It is. But it's also logical."

"How so?"

"Well, Darlene told me about her idea to have her wedding at a winery back in January when I started calling her. So I got this impulsive notion to buy a winery in Virginia. I figured if Darlene and Anthony had their wedding at my winery, I'd be able to see you, because you'd be there for sure."

"What if she didn't like your winery for her wedding?"

"She did like it. She had a lot of input into this," he said looking around.

"She did?"

"Yep. You see those sunflowers all over the place? And the bright ceramic vases? And the yellow on these walls? She also helped us design the new oaked chardonnay."

"*Really?*"

"Really. She said you like chardonnay, and the more oak, the better you'd like it. Jonathan's working on it, but it won't be ready for another year or so."

"What is it called?"

"What would you like it to be called?"

"*Secrets.*"

He searched her face for irony in her remark and asked "You forgive me?"

"I had no right to be upset with you. I am the one who needs to ask forgiveness, Mike."

He leaned down to kiss her.

"Wait!"

She wanted to have all the details cleared up before giving her full heart away.

"What?"

He would wait for the rest of his life if she had asked him.

"So how did you and Darlene keep this winery thing under wraps all this time?"

"Darlene and Anthony approached the owners of the Lotus Winery for me, and then we started negotiating. One of my property lawyers and I flew out with a friend who owns a winery in Sonoma, and we knew it would be a good investment. Darlene's fiancé helped us with the details and we finalized the deal from California. I hired the resident winemaker, Andreas, and Jonathan agreed to come on board because I didn't know a lick about making wine. Andreas kept on a few of the employees that had worked with the previous owner, and then he hired some others, like you."

"Did he know I was me?"

"No. That was purely coincidental. Ellie didn't know it was you either. Ellie gave him your number, apparently, and he called you. He was impressed with you and hired you. Then Darlene and I got nervous about Ellie finding out who you were, or you finding out about me."

"How would we find out?"

"Sooner or later you would get curious about why you hadn't met the owner, right?"

"That's true. I *was* curious, because Andreas never mentioned you by name or said much about you. He just referred to you as 'the boss'. And Elizabeth, I mean *Ellie*, never said your name either."

"Ellie wants to be independent, so she doesn't want anyone to know her father is the owner of the winery. It only would have been a matter of time before you would have found out about me, though, and I didn't want you to learn it from someone else."

"Is Ellie okay with you moving from California to Virginia?"

"Yes. She would have had to move anyway. She starts college on the east coast in the fall, so she would only be going back west for the summers. Even that wasn't guaranteed if she gets the summer internships at a design house in New York as she has planned."

"Is Moore College of Art in Pennsylvania?"

"Yes. It's only five hours from here, so she can drive home to Virginia on her winter and spring breaks a lot easier than to California. I'm keeping a condo in California, though, so she can always go back there to visit if she wants. She also has an open invitation to stay with Tyra and Sherrie in Los Angeles."

"Okay. I don't feel so guilty about your relocation to Virginia, then. But what if I had rejected your advances? You'd be stuck down here in this winery!"

"Are you kidding? I love it here, Rachel. I would have stayed here anyway. I was tired of the pressure of the law firm."

"This is pressure too, right? I mean, if the crops don't go as expected, if it rains too much—"

"Are you going to keep me waiting for a kiss forever?"

He pulled her close to his chest and looked down into her eyes.

"Well, I have one more—"

She never got around to her question.

Epilogue

DARLENE AND ANTHONY held their wedding ceremony and reception at Girasol Winery and Vineyards. It was a remarkable affair. So much so, Rachel and Michael decided to follow suit, and they got married at their winery the following summer.

Rachel continued teaching Spanish for the next two years and then retired to run the winery full-time with her husband. She learned to love secrets, as Michael surprised her on a regular basis with little gifts and strategically placed notes around the house. Oh yes, they built a house not too far from the winery across from the vineyards.

Michael travelled every now and then to California to look in on the law firm and visit some acclaimed vintners with whom he had been corresponding, but never without his wife.

Elizabeth went back to being Ellie. She graduated from Moore College of Art and began working for a design clothing line in New York City. She visited Virginia as much as possible, and always sported a new hair color to match her designer outfits. She moved in with a handsome struggling musician, a free spirit to compliment her own, and her dad kept close tabs on them.

Brandon received a full scholarship to North Carolina State, Chapel Hill, and graduated as an officer in the Marine Corps. He went on to be a Black Hawk and flew his helicopter for missions in the Middle East. Shortly thereafter he settled in Hawaii and met his future wife.

Andrew received a scholarship from the University of Virginia and went on to study medicine with a concentration in genetics and cancerous diseases. He never had another health issue resulting from the disease he had had as a boy, and neither did his twin daughters.

Oliver passed on shortly after Rachel and Michael got married, but not before fathering four puppies with a local neighbor's dog, all of which reside at El Girasol. Guests of the winery voted on names for the puppies after they were born. *Darth Vader* was the cutest puppy they had ever seen.

Secrets became a medal-winning Chardonnay.

Acknowledgments

I WOULD LIKE to express my gratitude to my daughter Lauren and my son Ricky for calling me on a regular basis so I won't be tempted to turn their bedrooms into gyms at our empty nest at home; I really don't want to work out every day. I miss you both and love you very much, as you know. I am so proud of whom you have become in your independence. I know about your quiet acts of kindness, your words of encouragement to friends and each other, and your compassion for those in need. I admire you, Lauren, for the twelve-plus hours you work every day, for never quitting in the face of adversity, and for making sure the job is done well. Your work ethic and perseverance amaze me. I love hearing all your stories during our mom and daughter outings to the mall; even the ones about being stranded in the snow storm while on business in Chicago, or diligently driving throughout the city trying to find jobs for each one of your employees when one of the shops was shut down. And I commend you, Ricky, for living and working in a foreign country, navigating through daily minutiae in a foreign language, and striving to be the professional baseball player you have dreamed of becoming. It was tough getting your call when you were working on the beach of the resort during the earthquake, with the possibility of a tsunami to follow; and the one when you were stranded out in the middle of nowhere after work at night with a broken car and no one to assist you; and the call you placed after carrying a six-foot baseball player from your team down a slippery mountain path, digging under a fence to get him to a car, and then rushing him to the hospital after breaking his leg. But never stop telling me your stories, either one of you, because I love you too much to not know the bad with the good. Moms can handle anything. Besides, I can follow you on Facebook.

To my husband Dave, who has given me the space to write and to be true to myself, I love you. You are the free spirit that makes me laugh and invites me to live life to its fullest, and I am grateful. You are kind and loving and understanding. I never know when flowers will appear on the counter in the kitchen, a little gift will appear on my dresser, or tickets to a fun event will appear in my mailbox. You are unpredictable, and I love your surprises! I look forward to our eventual retirement and to living near the beach. Or the mountains. Or down south. You really need to make up your mind.

To my wonderful step-sons Justin and Matt, thank you for adopting me and accepting me into your worlds. You are smart and caring young men who are definitely on the path to a promising future. Justin, it is always fun listening to your stories about playing drums with Youth Encounter and in gigs all over the east coast. I can't wait to go to your wedding this summer in Maine; it will be so much fun! Matt, your dad and I always enjoy your stories about fish-ing trips, skiing, playing football and baseball, and we enjoy listening to you on the guitar!

I send my love to all my siblings who have given me their constant support over the years: Ginger, Hono, Margaret, Robin, Patti, Katie, and Stevie, and to their significant others and their children. We've been through a lot of crap in our lives, haven't we? You are all some of the strongest people I have had the honor of knowing. Your resiliency astounds me.

And finally, I would like to thank my real-life friend Darlene, a counselor indeed, for her patience not only with me, but with the hundreds of students who she has helped over the years. We have laughed with some of those students and cried with others. Their stories are incredible. You are a good listener, Darlene, just like your character. I know sometimes you need to be tough. Be nice to me. And by the way, I had a great time at your wedding to your wonderful husband Tony. You seriously need to teach me to dance.

About the Author

CHERYL HOLDEFER RESIDES IN Columbia, Maryland, with her husband and their four children on any given day. Especially on days when they smell Dave's crab cakes baking or Cheryl's pumpkin cookies in the oven. Or maybe they just want to see the dog.

She is a former Spanish and French teacher, adjunct faculty member for Johns Hopkins University, and she is currently a high school Assistant Principal.

She was recently highlighted in *Howard Magazine* as the author of *Victoria's Run*, a story about a single parent who struggles with the details of her daily life while training for the Olympic Marathon. When the protagonist's goals are obstructed by misfortune, and a love relationship crumbles, she struggles to make sense of it all. In a surprise ending, the protagonist is faced with complex decisions and she finds strength and resolve in the power of a dream. Find *Victoria's Run* in paperback or on Kindle at amazon.com.

For more information and updates on Cheryl's Books, visit:

FACEBOOK
https://www.facebook.com/pages/Cheryl-Holdefer/132424563596673

OTHER TITLES BY CHERYL HOLDEFER

LIKE MANY SINGLE parents, Victoria Richards has to deal with the details of everyday life---raising two children, working and paying bills, managing a home---even as she contemplates realizing her dream to compete in the Olympic Marathon. An unexpected love interest surfaces, and she dares to fall in love completely. When the path to her dreams is suddenly obstructed by misfortune, Victoria is crushed.

She is invited to Puerto Rico to organize a major race, and in doing so, she hopes to overcome the difficulties she has encountered and begin her life again. In a surprise ending, Victoria is faced with some complex decisions to make, and she finds strength and renewed resolve from the power of a dream.

Set against the backdrop of two beautiful countries, Denmark and Puerto Rico, Cheryl Holdefer delivers an emotional story of love, loss, courage, and determination. Her book is an affirmation of not setting limits to what can be achieved.